A Taste for Adventure

by

Jane Ritzenthaler

Copyright ©2022 Jane Ritzenthaler
All Rights Reserved

CHAPTER ONE

"How about this one," Grant Thompson said, excitement in his voice as he read from the website on his laptop. "Explore the Serengeti during its wildebeest migration and photograph big game while enjoying sophisticated and intimate tented camp accommodations."

Kate McCracken sucked in a breath and exhaled it slowly.

"Ah...tents? Seriously? On our honeymoon?"

"But just look at this," he said, undaunted. He swiveled his laptop on the kitchen breakfast bar so she could take a look at the images. She had to admit it was a far cry from the two-man popup that she remembered from her childhood. It showed a large wooden platform with a living space open to a deck, topped with soaring canvas sections to protect against the sun and elements.

"Um...okay, I guess we could consider it..." she said, her voice trailing off. But then her eyes landed on the price, and she screeched. "Eight thousand dollars! *Each!!*" She began shaking her head. "No, Grant, that's crazy! We'd be paying for it until our tenth anniversary!"

The tall, handsome Sheriff pulled Kate into his arms and ran his fingers through her curly blond hair.

"It's that Scottish heritage," he laughed, looking into the green eyes that flashed sparks of gold when she was excited or angry. "Alright, then, what would you like to do? Not that it really matters," he said, one side of his mouth curling up into a grin. "I may not let you get too far away from my arms anyway."

She blushed and gave him a gentle kiss, then turned back to her laptop. Their wedding was less than six weeks away, on the second Saturday in August. A bit late to be planning a honeymoon, but fortunately, the wedding itself would be simple. As weddings went these days, anyway. Since Kate's parents had both passed away, and her only sibling, Ned, was a SEAL, she was relying on Grant's mother to help plan the event. It would be a simple affair, held in the rose garden in the Thompson's back yard, which overlooked a golf course. Celia was quite creative, and Kate knew she could relax and let her future mother-in-law and sister-in-law, Paula, do their thing. All she had to do was find a dress, and show up.

"Frankly, Grant, I'm leaning toward a cruise," she said, clicking on the site she had been perusing. "A floating hotel, no changing rooms, or packing and unpacking, and everything's included. We can eat as often and as much as we'd like. And they have couple's massages in the spa..."

Grant scooted his bar stool closer to look over her shoulder. "All right, now you're talking my language!"

"Here's one, a seven-day Alaskan cruise. We'd fly to Anchorage, then sail the inland passage with stops in three ports, and end up in Vancouver, Canada. And look at the price! Even with a balcony suite, it would be less than three thousand for both of us!"

Grant cocked his head to the side and gave a slow nod.

"That does look good," he agreed. "Especially since we're here in Napa Valley, the flights from San Francisco probably wouldn't be that bad." Kate gave an un-ladylike snort.

"Compared to flights to Africa, I guess!" She turned back to her computer. "This is on Princess. I have friends that have sailed on them, and they think they're top notch. Plus, we wouldn't want to be on one of those "fun" cruise lines, with hundreds of screaming children running about."

"Definitely not," he agreed with a chuckle. "We'll wait until we have some of our own screaming children to book one of those." He pulled out his credit card and handed it to her. "Let's do it."

While Kate completed the reservation, Grant stood and walked to the counter to pour himself another cup of coffee. He loved the vintage home in old town Napa that Kate's late father had remodeled, transforming the original bungalow into a family home by finishing the attic into two bedrooms, and building an addition that housed the master suite. They planned to live in her house after they were married, and he had recently put his condo on the market.

He looked over at Kate, and for the umpteenth time that day, thanked the Lord for bringing her back into his life. Grant and her older brother had been classmates in high school, and Ned's kid sister had obviously had a crush on him. When he was over at the house, helping Ned work on his car, she would hang around and try to 'help.' She never thought he'd noticed her, but oh yes, he'd noticed all right. But she was only 13 then...and after he'd left for college, their lives went in different directions. At eighteen, she'd run off and married John Bateman, only to find herself divorced and devastated two years later.

And then there was Lisa. Then a deputy with the Napa Valley Sheriff's Department, he had been engaged to marry the rookie. But she had been killed in the line of duty, and he still carried around guilt for not being able to prevent her death that day.

Two years ago, Kate had returned from a job as a photojournalist with a major San Francisco paper to take care of her dying mother. Alice had passed six months later, and Kate had decided to stay. While working freelance for the Napa Valley

Register, she had stumbled upon a murder in a local winery. Grant had been part of the investigation that night, and the chance encounter led to their friendship being rekindled.

"There," she said triumphantly, "all set. I'll print out the confirmation details. But we only have a week to select our day trips from the ports we'll be stopping in."

"Okay, send me the link, and I'll start looking, too. Then we can compare our favorites."

"Will do." She glanced at the clock on the wall. "Yikes, it's almost 9:30. I told Dan I'd stop by this morning to help him select photos for an updated wine country tour page on the website."

"Go on, then...I'll clean up the breakfast stuff and lock up." She rose from her seat at the breakfast bar and gave him a hug.

"Thank you...you're definitely a keeper."

Fifteen minutes later, she pulled into the parking lot of the nondescript building that housed the Napa Valley Register. The bell on the door dinged as she pushed it open, and Peggy looked up from behind the front desk. The older woman with frizzy salt and pepper hair gave Kate a big grin.

"Hi Kate, how's the bride-to-be?"

"Trying not to stress, thank you!" she laughed.

"Dan's expecting you; head on back." Kate walked down the short hall and tapped on the frame of the open doorway.

"Kate!" the 50-something editor greeted her, waving her in. "How are the wedding plans coming?"

Kate sighed as she sank into a chair in front of the cluttered desk.

"I'm leaving the wedding details to Celia and Paula; I probably won't remember much of that day, anyway. But Grant and I finally settled on where to go on our honeymoon. An Alaskan cruise."

"Excellent choice, my dear," he said. "Edna and I did that for our 25th anniversary. Loved it."

"Now we have to select excursions from each of the three ports," Kate commented. "And there are lots to choose from."

"Well, there's one definitely not to miss," Dan said. "A floatplane ride from Juneau over the glaciers, and landing at Taku Lodge for a mouth-watering salmon bake. A bit pricey, but well worth it."

"Oh, that sounds like fun! I'll have to check it out." Taking a sticky note from Dan's desk, she scribbled a note on it and put it in her purse.

"Alright, Kate, here are the photos you took that I'm planning on using on the updated Napa Wine Taste website." She got up and came around behind his desk, pulling a stool up next to him. They spent the next half hour trying different layouts until they both pronounced it good.

She left the newspaper office with a renewed thankfulness that the Lord had brought her back to Napa. Not only did she love her job, but she was about to embark on the adventure of her lifetime with the man she loved.

CHAPTER TWO

The weeks flew by, and before she had time to even get nervous, the wedding day had arrived. The rehearsal the evening before had been more about food and fellowship and not much about practicing the simple ceremony.

Kate was getting dressed in the master bedroom, assisted by Celia and Jason's wife, Paula. After several frustrating trips in search of the perfect dress at a reasonable price, she had finally found just the right one at Nordstrom's Rack. Standing in front of the mirror wearing the pale pink sheath dress with spaghetti straps, she raised her arms so Celia could slip the lacy long-sleeved layered overdress over her head. There were tiny pearl buttons closing the back, and the dress hugged her curves and flared below her knees. Kate's curls were pulled back on one side, fastened with a flowered clip. Kate slipped on her matching pink heels and surveyed herself in the full-length mirror.

That's when the butterflies started.

It was really happening...she was about to marry her childhood crush.

A light knock was heard at the door. "It's about time, ladies," Art called through the closed door. Kate inhaled a steadying breath and took the beautiful bouquet of pink and white flowers that Celia had fashioned. She gave a nod and a quivery smile, and Celia opened the door. Her brother Ned stood waiting, wearing his dress Navy uniform.

"Wow, Sis, you look beautiful!"

"Hey, don't sound so surprised," Paula said, poking him in the shoulder. Ned offered his arm to Kate, and they followed Paula to the sliding glass doors open to the patio and rose garden below.

Kate caught her breath when she saw Grant, tall and handsome in his pearl-gray jacket and charcoal pants standing next to Pastor Scott under the rose arbor. Soft music started playing, and Paula led the way out onto the patio and down the steps. Paula joined her husband Jason, the best man, and Ned placed Kate's hand into Grant's.

The scene faded as if in a dream, and Kate and Grant were aware of nothing except each other. They barely heard Scott addressing the small gathering, and the pastor had to prompt Grant twice to say his vows. His voice broke as he began to speak:

"Kate, I have loved you since you were a freckled-face teenager, and today I vow to love and cherish you for the rest of our lives. Our house will be one of prayer, and the Lord will be the center of our marriage." Kate blinked back tears when it was her turn to speak:

"Grant, I vow to honor and respect you as my husband and the head of our household, and to love and be faithful to you for the rest of our lives."

They slipped the simple gold rings on each other's fingers, and bowed their heads as Scott prayed over them.

"Grant, you may kiss your wife!" Scott grinned as Grant gently took Kate's face in his hands and kissed her tenderly. The guests clapped, and a joyous song began playing. Kate started giggling, and unsuccessfully tried to regain her composure as they walked hand and hand back up to the patio.

The afternoon seemed to be on fast-forward, zooming through champagne toasts and cake cutting, and as the sun began setting behind the hills, the couple was showered with birdseed as they ran toward their car. Grant opened the passenger door so Kate could slide in, then ran around and jumped in behind the wheel. He turned and gave her a huge grin.

"We did it!

CHAPTER THREE

Sunday morning, Kate rose from the rumpled bed where her new husband lay sleeping and walked to the window. Gently parting the curtains, she gazed over the Golden Gate bridge poking above the fog in the early morning light.

So peaceful.

She let out a satisfied sigh, remembering the night before.

Grant. Her husband. Her amazing lover.

Thank You, Lord, she whispered. *You have indeed redeemed what the locusts ate...*

She heard a rustling behind her, and soon an arm snaked around her waist, pulling her close to his naked chest.

"Good morning, beautiful." Grant nuzzled her neck and breathed in her scent.

She turned and nestled into his chest. She had been delighted to discover a small patch of curly blond hair there, and laughed when it tickled her nose.

"And good morning to you, husband!"

"Mmmm...love that. 'Husband'. I probably should be beating my chest and letting out a war whoop..."

Kate laughed, pulling back and looking him in his still sleepy eyes. "Want to join me in the shower?"

She felt his response.

"You know it."

Two hours later, they checked out of the hotel and jumped into the hotel shuttle to the airport. The fog had lifted, and the sun was sparkling on the bay. They were left off at Alaska Airlines, and Grant tipped the shuttle driver before grabbing the handles of both bags and beginning to drag them toward the terminal doors.

"Hey now," Kate said, taking the handle of her bright yellow suitcase. "I'm a liberated woman, remember?"

"Ah yes, how could I forget..." he smiled, relinquishing the suitcase.

They checked in at the kiosk, and were soon standing in line at the security check point.

"Hurry up and wait," Kate said with a resigned sigh. "I'm not sure we're any safer now than back in the day my parents were flying off to Chile, with nary a question thrown at them."

"Really? Chile?" He turned to look at her, eyebrows raised. "I don't think you ever mentioned that. Were you along?"

"Oh no, I was just a little tyke, and sent off to Aunt Alice while they were away. But I do remember the slides...hours and hours of them...when they got back."

"So it's on your bucket list?" Grant asked, inching forward in the line.

"Maybe...but I think Europe would top my list. How about you?"

"Definitely. Austria...Germany...Switzerland..."

"And don't forget Paris in the spring," Kate interjected. "Maybe for our 10th anniversary?"

He shook his head with a frown. "No way, my dear...sounds perfect for our first anniversary."

"But that would be in August...definitely not spring in Paris!"

"A mere technicality," he said, planting a kiss on her cheek. "Then it will be our 20-month anniversary. I mean, how many people do you know who celebrate that?"

She laughed as they advanced to the dour faced man who was waving at them from the podium. He scrutinized their faces, comparing them to their passports, and waved them towards the lines at the conveyor belts.

After partially disrobing and being subjected to the x-ray machines, they were soon on their way to their gate.

They settled into seats at Gate 17, with a half hour wait before boarding would begin. Kate loved people-watching at airports, and San Francisco had a little of everything to offer. She marveled at the languages that floated around her, and the colorful outfits that accompanied them. She recalled the Scripture that mandated the Gospel be taken to all the world. Until each tribe and people group had heard that He had come...

"Clark just sent me a text," Grant said, disrupting her musings. "There was a break-in at Jumpin' Java."

"What?" she exclaimed, sitting up in the chair. Her good friend Ariana owned the coffee shop in Napa. A recovering addict, she now led a Celebrate Recovery group at their church. "Is Ariana okay?"

"Yes. Apparently, she wasn't there...it happened sometime during the night."

"Just a robbery, then?" Kate asked.

"Maybe..." Grant frowned as he scrolled through the text. "But Clark says a note was left on the counter. 'This is just the beginning.'" He looked up at Kate. "I don't like the sound of that."

Kate blanched and grabbed her phone from her purse. She found Ariana's number and punched the call icon. Her friend answered on the third ring.

"Kate? Why are you calling me...you're on your honeymoon, for goodness sake!"

"So? Grant said your place was broken into last night. And that a threatening note was left. Are you all right?"

"Guess so...a bit shaken up, I'll admit. When I opened up the store this morning, I knew somebody had been there...the back door off the parking lot was open. I called 911 immediately, didn't even go in."

"That was smart," Kate acknowledged. "Grant said a note was found..." She heard a sigh from her friend.

"Yes..."

"Do you have any idea what it means?" Kate's forehead scrunched as she leaned over the phone in her lap.

"No idea. But with my background...who knows?"

Kate glanced at Grant, who was hearing the conversation.

"The Chief Deputy Sheriff, Clark, is handling it." Grant nodded in agreement. "So don't stress...and we'll be back in a week. And remember...God's got this!"

"Thank you, Kate, I know He does! Have a great time on your cruise. Talk to you when you get back."

Kate disconnected the call and looked at Grant.

"I don't like the sound of that at all. Maybe we should head back..."

"Not a chance," he said, grabbing her hand. "I totally trust Clark, and there's no way I'm cancelling our honeymoon!"

Kate looked into those hazel eyes and melted.

"No...no, I definitely don't want that either. But promise me that you'll stay in touch with Clark..."

"Done," he said, drawing her into a side hug. "I care about Ariana as much as you do."

The gate agent was announcing the boarding of their flight, and when their group was called, they arose and got in line. They had chosen seats toward the back, behind the wings, and as they took their seats Kate was delighted to look out her window seat at the tarmac which would soon give way to mountains.

This was the beginning...of a new chapter in her life.

And Kate was ready.

CHAPTER FOUR

The shuttle deposited them at the train station in Anchorage, a mountain of suitcases in the parking lot, awaiting their arrival. Kate breathed in the clean mountain air, marveling at it all. The train would take them to the port in Whittier, where they would board their cruise ship. The air was cool, even in August. Clouds were forming overhead as they boarded the sleek silver train. Based on advice from a friend who had done this trip before, they took seats on the right side of the train. Soon they were on their way.

Kate's nose was pressed to the window as the train wound its way between mountains and water. Grant was snuggled up behind her, looking over her shoulder.

"This is amazing..." she exclaimed, squeezing his leg.

"If this is how great God's world looks in its fallen state, I can hardly wait to see it when He recreates it!"

She laughed, turning to face him and planting a kiss on his lips.

"You know how much I love you, right?"

A smile spread across his face.

"Yes, I certainly do."

Rain was falling at a gentle but steady pace when they arrived at the port of Whittier. Ahead lay their cruise ship.

"Oh my goodness, it's huge!" Kate exclaimed as they walked toward the gangplank.

"It's a small city," Grant agreed. "And our home for the next seven days."

They were greeted and directed to their stateroom, on an upper deck. Kate slipped the card into the lock and opened the door, gasping as she saw the balcony overlooking the water.

"Oh my, this is wonderful!"

"Good choice, wife!" Grant exclaimed. He opened the slider and stepped out onto the narrow balcony. She came alongside him and put her arm around him.

"This is so beautiful..."

"Better than an African safari?" he said with a teasing tone in his voice.

"Well...different, anyway. And definitely cheaper!"

The ship was set to sail at 5:00, and they spent the next few minutes unpacking. When the horns began to blast, they returned to the balcony and watched as the ship slowly left port. The rain continued, but it didn't dampen their spirits.

"What time does the sun set up here, anyway?" Grant asked. He was sure his bride had already checked that out.

"Not until about 10:00," she replied. "And sunrise is around 6:00."

"That will feel weird," he said, gazing out into the mist. "Okay, Miss Almanac, what's it like in the middle of winter?"

"Only about 6 hours of daylight," she said with a smirk. "The sun isn't up until 10:00 and sets around 4:00. And that's here in Anchorage – further north, you get that infamous midnight sun."

"Don't think I could handle that," Grant said with a frown. He turned at the railing and faced her. "From what our itinerary says, we're on our own for dinner tonight. Formal dining doesn't start until tomorrow. How about we go check out this floating hotel and find something to eat?"

"Sounds good to me. I'll just freshen up and be right with you." She entered the tiny bathroom and touched up her makeup, then ran her fingers through her curls and called it good. She paused to smile at herself in the mirror.

Mrs. Grant Thompson.

Amazing.

Holding hands, they wandered through the ship, glancing at the schematic provided by the cruise line. Grant decided it would be way too easy to get lost, with all the levels and venues. They passed the casino, an art gallery, signs pointing to the main theater stage, and found themselves at the top of a grand flight of stairs descending in an atrium through four levels. Shops and restaurants lined each mezzanine.

"There's an elevator over there," Grant said, motioning to the glass cubicle gliding to the lower level.

"No way," Kate said, pulling him forward. "I want the full experience!"

After peeking into three restaurants and viewing the menus posted at the door, they chose an Italian restaurant and were quickly escorted to a table with an ocean view.

"This reminds me a bit of Jumpin' Java," Kate remarked as she looked around. Her friend's coffee shop and deli looked more like the garden in an Italian villa than your typical sleek coffee shop, with arbors covered with artificial grape vines, and frescos on the interior walls.

"It does, doesn't it?" Grant commented, spreading the linen napkin on his lap. Kate could hear soft Italian opera music in the background.

After perusing the menu, Grant settled on the lasagna, and Kate chose the veal scaloppini. He picked up the wine list and raised his eyebrows. "White?"

"Yes, that sounds good. Maybe a Pino Grigio?" She stifled her next comment, which was to be a reminder that alcohol wasn't included in their cruise price. *Good grief*, she scolded herself, *I'm on my honeymoon!* And they had already had The Discussion about finances. There would be no 'his and hers' money. Grant had been elected Sheriff in a special election two months before after the existing Sheriff had died of a heart attack. Grant's income would provide for their major living expenses, and Kate's could be used for incidentals, such as the landscaping she wanted to do in the backyard. Any expenditure exceeding $500 would be discussed and agreed upon beforehand.

The waiter brought their wine, smoothly uncorking it and allowing Grant to taste it before pouring it into both wineglasses. He set the bottle into a stone chiller and took their orders.

Grant lifted his glass in a toast and his eyes sparkled as he looked into hers.

"Here's to my beautiful bride of...26 hours, 32 minutes," he said, glancing at his watch. "May this be the beginning of many, many years...I want to grow old with you, Kate. And watch our grandchildren grow."

Kate smiled in return, lifting her glass to touch his.

"Grandchildren...that would require children first, right?" she teased.

"Yes indeedy...and at our advanced ages, we'd better get started!"

After their delicious dinners, they strolled out onto the deck and watched the sun begin to dip into the ocean. The rain clouds had moved off, promising a night of starlit skies. Kate hadn't brought a jacket to dinner, but thankfully, small blankets were available on the deck chairs, and Grant scooped one up and wrapped it around her shoulders. They leaned on the railing, Grant's arms holding her close.

"Did you ever think we'd be here...as husband and wife, I mean?" Kate asked. "All those years ago, I was just your best friend's little sister..."

"And you were the cutest freckle-faced pest I'd ever met," he replied, planting a kiss in her hair. "I actually imagined that one day we'd be together. But then you ran off with that jerk when you were 18. I thought that was the end of it."

She heaved a sigh and snuggled closer as she remembered those crazy years.

"I thought he was Prince Charming...but finding him two years later with my supposed best friend, *in our bed*, for heaven's sake..." she trailed off, shaking her head as if to banish the memories.

"But then our paths crossed again at Tres Cruces winery when you found the body of the murdered gossip blogger." He stroked her cheek and turned her face towards him. "I knew in that moment I would never let you get away again." He drew her into a passionate kiss that took their breaths away.

"Why don't we check out the view from our balcony?" she said with a smirk.

"Excellent idea, Mrs. Thompson. Lead the way."

CHAPTER FIVE

Grant awoke the next morning to the sound of the shower running in their bathroom. He rolled out of bed and pulled on his pajama bottoms, glancing at the clock. Almost 7:30. He opened the curtains to a view of fog rolling over the ocean, the early-morning sun peeking through now and then. The shower turned off, and he walked over to the bathroom door.

"Could I interest anyone in a cup of coffee?" The door popped open and water dripped on his bare toes.

"Silly question," she laughed, grabbing a towel for her wet hair. He leaned in to plant a kiss on her cheek, then turned towards the small breakfast bar.

"Coming right up."

He dropped a dark roast pod into the personal sized machine and watched it fill the mug, then repeated the process with one for himself.

"Mmmm, that smells wonderful," Kate remarked from the bathroom.

"I should have thought to order room service for breakfast," Grant apologized when he brought her the steaming mug.

"That's okay, I think I'd rather go to the buffet. The photos on the website looked pretty impressive."

Grant jumped in the shower while Kate finished getting ready, and twenty minutes later they were in search of the cafeteria. As they entered the huge room, he had to admit it did look amazing. The center of the room held several buffet tables holding hot foods in steam trays, towers of fresh fruit, cereals, waffle makers, an omelet station...and a coffee bar with the typical specialty drinks. Tables were scattered on the perimeter, with slanted windows showcasing the Hubbard Glacier the ship was gliding past.

Grant groaned as he surveyed the sumptuous display.

"Which deck is it again where we can jog around the entire ship?"

"That would be the Lido deck," Kate laughed, "where we're headed later today. But not to jog. The Lotus spa is there, too." She picked up two trays, handing one to Grant, and walked over to the buffet holding the waffle and omelet makers. A young man dressed all in white was skillfully flipping an omelet for another passenger and then gracefully slid it onto the plate.

"Ooh, that looks yummy," Kate said as she stepped up.

"What would you like, Miss?" he asked, pouring eggs into a prepared skillet.

"How about spinach, tomatoes, mushrooms...and feta?"

He nodded and picked up small dishes holding the requested ingredients, sprinkling them on top of the bubbling eggs.

"Oh, and bacon," she added.

"And you, sir?"

"I'm more of a Belgian waffle man," Grant replied, walking to the other end of the table where another white-clad server held forth over four steaming waffle makers.

Kate's omelet was finished first, so she took her plate to an available table, stopping on the way to add crispy hash browns and rye toast. Grant followed, with bowls of fresh berries and whipped cream.

"I think I could get used to this," he murmured as a server appeared, pouring coffee into their mugs. He took Kate's outstretched hand and offered up a quick blessing.

"Well, enjoy it while it lasts," she replied, digging into her omelet. "Next week it's back to cold cereal and store-bought orange juice."

"*That's* what I forgot," he said, jumping up. "The freshly squeezed stuff. Want some?" When she nodded, he wound his way to the beverage bar and poured two glasses from the dispenser.

As he settled back into his chair, he gazed out the windows at the scenery.

"This is what they call a sailing day, right?" he asked.

"Exactly. We're passing by the Hubbard Glacier, and will be at sea all day. That's why I thought it was a good time to enjoy the spa."

"The couple's massage, right?" he asked, wiggling his eyebrows.

"Yes, but remember, there will be two masseuses...we won't be alone." He feigned a tragic look.

"What time is our appointment?"

"I scheduled it at 2:30."

"You mean we have to eat again before that? Maybe we *should* do the jogging thing."

"I was thinking more of a leisurely stroll...pausing now and then to sit on a deck chair, covered with a lap robe, and gazing out to sea."

"Wow...and try not to wonder what's going on at the office," he muttered.

"Grant!" she groaned, with an exaggerated eye roll, "we're on our honeymoon! I'm sure Napa County won't fall apart before you get back."

"Just kidding," he laughed. "I'm looking forward to this week being all about us. After all, I had to wait years and years for it."

"Actually, I wouldn't mind if you checked in with Clark," Kate admitted. "I'm concerned about Ariana."

He smiled at her and said, "I know. I am too. I'll give him a call while we're sitting on those deck chairs."

They finished their breakfasts and lingered over a second cup of coffee. By 9:30, they had stopped by their cabin to retrieve jackets, and headed up to the Lido deck. Other passengers were strolling the wide wooden deck, and some were even jogging. They stood at the railing, watching the wake curling away from the ship into the dissipating fog, and in the distance snow-capped mountains rose from the sea. Kate took out her iPhone and snapped a photo of the front edge of the glacier as it met the ocean. Then she grabbed Grant and turned him around, lining up a selfie.

"Smile! This will be on Facebook in a few moments."

"Guess we have to prove we were really here," he mumbled, hugging his bride close to his side and smiling into the camera.

They did stroll around the deck a full circle, pausing to chat with an older couple celebrating their 50th wedding anniversary.

"Fifty years," Kate whispered as they walked away. "Do you think..."

"What, that we'll get there?" Grant asked, circling her with his arm. "Why not? We'll only be...uh, 80 something..."

"I'll be 82...and you, God willing, will be 86!"

"I don't think I want to see that selfie," he laughed. "If they even have Facebook then."

"Who knows, it might be holograms by then. Even scarier."

Grant steered her over to a pair of deck chairs, and helped her settle in, tucking the lap robe around her. He planted a lingering kiss on her lips before scooting his chair as close to hers as possible. He reached over and held out his hand. She grasped it and looked into his eyes.

"I love you, Grant Thompson. To 80-something and beyond."

His eyes misted slightly, and he squeezed her hand.

"And beyond...into eternity."

Before they knew it, it was time for lunch. Still feeling full from the breakfast buffet, they chose a small deli and had salads. Grant had indeed called Clark while they were seated on the Lido deck, but the deputy had nothing new to report on the break-in at Jumpin' Java. They had canvassed the area, but no one had seen or heard anything during the night. Collecting fingerprints at a coffee shop was virtually pointless, but they had done it anyway, especially around the back door and the counter where the note had been left.

At 2:30, Kate and Grant followed the signs to the Lotus Spa, and entered into the waiting area. A wall of water coursed down a rock surface behind the reception desk, and tropical plants were placed around the area. Soft music played in the background, and Kate breathed in the subtle incense.

"Welcome to the Lotus Spa," chirped the young woman with dark hair swept up to one side and pinned with a flower.

"Thank you," Kate replied, stepping up to the counter. "Mr. and Mrs. Thompson. We have an appointment for a massage."

"Yes, Clarissa will escort you," she replied, gesturing to the woman who appeared at the entrance to a hallway.

Clarissa was in her 20s, wearing a sarong. Grant gave Kate a wink as they followed her into a room. Two massage tables were in front, with dressing rooms at the back.

"You may disrobe in the rooms, and put on the garments you will find in there."

Kate smiled at Grant and opened the curtain into one of the cubicles. She took off all her clothing, and donned the pink wrap-around terrycloth coverup. When she exited, she saw Grant was already standing next to one table, wearing a gray abbreviated version of the coverup around his waist. A man and a woman were standing at the foot of each table. As he eyed them, Grant made a decision. He'd take the male masseuse...

But then the woman gestured to him.

"My name is Gina. Please lie down on your stomach on the table." He looked at Kate, and she shrugged. He obliged, carefully placing himself on the table. He turned his head to watch Kate being guided onto her table by Herb. They smiled at each other as the soothing massages began.

And Grant had to admit it was soothing...and then some. Gina spread fragrant oil on his back and began kneading his muscles...muscles he hadn't even realized needed to be kneaded. He heard small sounds of pleasure coming from Kate's direction, and opened his eyes to watch her. *Dear Lord*, he thought, *thank you for giving me this amazing woman.*

After the massages, warm rocks were placed on their backs, and they were left to rest for a few minutes. They gazed at each other, words unnecessary.

Next, they were led into a room with a large jacuzzi, and thankfully left alone. Dropping their towels, they slid into the steaming water.

"That was incredible," Grant murmured, reaching his hand towards Kate.

"Yes, it was," she replied, grasping his hand. "I can't remember when I was that relaxed before."

"Okay then, this goes on our favorites list..."

After a few minutes, he turned toward her, pulling her into his arms.

CHAPTER SIX

It was a wonder they even made it to dinner that evening. But this was the first night when they would meet their assigned tablemates for the rest of the cruise, and Kate insisted they had to go.

They entered the dining room, and were directed to table 14. It was a table for eight, and six chairs were already occupied. They slid into the last two chairs, and offered smiles to the others. The couple to their right was younger than they were, and of Asian descent. Kate, as a journalist, was used to initiating conversations.

"Hi, I'm Kate, and this is my husband, Grant. We're from California, and on our honeymoon."

The dark-haired woman next to her responded.

"How wonderful! I'm Aiko, and this is Kenji."

Grant turned to the others at the table. He met the eyes of a man, probably in his 50s, with dark hair graying at the temples.

"Arnold Caldwell. My wife, Julia. We're celebrating our 30th anniversary." Grant's eyes traveled to the young woman on his other side.

"Mindy Marshall," the auburn-haired woman said. "I'm Mr. Caldwell's Administrative Assistant." She hesitatingly gestured to the muscular man at her right.

"Sal Dimario." He thrust out a meaty hand and shook Grant's.

The server appeared at the table and asked if anyone would like a beverage. Glances moved around the table, and everyone chose their preferences. Grant and Kate decided on a Merlot, while Mr. Caldwell ordered champagne. The Asian couple ordered a white wine, and Sal asked for a dark beer. Mindy only wanted sparkling water with a lime.

Dinner selections were made, wine was delivered and uncorked, and attempts were made to become acquainted.

Aiko spoke first.

"This is so exciting...we've never been on a cruise before. How about all of you?"

Kate had to smile at the enthusiastic comment, and turned to the young woman. She had long dark hair, and her husband had closely cropped hair and a neatly trimmed beard.

"First time for us, too. We're from Napa, California...where are you from?"

"Manilla. I teach English, and my husband is with a brokerage firm." She turned to beam at him. "This cruise was his reward for bringing in the most clients last year."

"I work for the local paper, and Grant is the county Sheriff," Kate replied. She didn't notice the side glance Sal gave Arnold. Kate's gaze fell on the older couple.

"I'm with Caldwell Industries. My wife, Julia, is involved with several non-profits in our area." Julia sat mute, twirling her wine glass while her husband spoke. Kate noted that Arnold Caldwell was assertive, a bit like a politician, with his polished presentation and photographic smile.

"And you work for Mr. Caldwell?" Kate asked the woman at his elbow. She was an attractive woman, probably in her mid-twenties.

"I do," she responded simply. She glanced at Sal and unfolded her napkin, smoothing it on her lap. He placed his arm across the back of her chair, and gave the rest of the table a close-lipped smile.

The server reappeared, and choices were made for dinner. Ensuing conversation centered on the cruise, the weather, and what everyone had chosen for port excursions.

After dinner, everyone went their separate ways. Kate watched the Filipino couple heading to the auditorium, and the Caldwells settled into club chairs in the main lounge in the atrium. He immediately pulled out his phone and began scrolling, while his wife extracted a Kindle from her purse and opened it.

"What do you have in mind, Kate?" He took her hand as they strolled through the atrium. She gazed up to one of the mezzanines.

"Let's check out some of the shops...I'd like to find a necklace to wear tomorrow night."

"What's tomorrow night?"

"Formal night. I brought that slinky black dress you like, but I didn't have the right thing to wear with it. I've never been one for wearing a lot of jewelry, but that dress definitely needs something."

"Okay, let's see what we can find." They climbed the curved staircase to the next level, where several boutiques were located. They passed shops offering clothing and items with the Princess logo, souvenir shops, and finally came upon a jewelry store. Two large crystal chandeliers were suspended in the shop, causing everything in the glass display cases to sparkle. They were quickly approached by a young woman in a black silk suit.

"Good evening...may I help you find something?"

"Yes, my bride is looking for something special to wear with a provocatively low-cut black dress." Kate blushed and punched him in the arm. The saleswoman gave Kate a knowing smile.

"A necklace, then, with matching earrings?" she asked.

"Yes, and something...simple. I'm not one for gaudy jewelry."

The woman, whose nametag indicated her name was Susan, looked Kate over, from head to toe. She took in the curly strawberry blond hair, green eyes, and lithe build.

"I think I have just the perfect thing." She gestured, and they followed her to the adjoining case. Unlocking the back of the case, she withdrew a small bust displaying a necklace consisting of an intricate gold chain on which hung a beautiful sapphire surrounded by tiny diamonds. The earrings were smaller replicas.

"Oh, that's beautiful!" Kate exclaimed. She reached for the pendant and let the light dance off it. But then she turned over the price tag and paled. "Uh...no, I'm sorry, but..."

Grant reached over and gently took her hand.

"We'll take it. It will look beautiful on her."

Tears welled up in Kate's eyes as Grant pulled out his credit card and handed it to Susan. She replied with a smile, and turned to ring up the sale.

"But Grant..." Kate stuttered.

"But nothing," he replied, firmly. "I realize I'm paying more than I would if we weren't on this cruise ship, but we *are* on our honeymoon, and I frankly don't care." A slow smile spread across Kate's face, and she leaned in to give him a tender kiss.

"I am so blessed to have you, you know."

"No more than I am to have you, my love."

CHAPTER SEVEN

The following morning, Grant and Kate once again indulged in the extravagant breakfast buffet. This time, she chose moist scrambled eggs, and Grant opted for French toast. Seated at a table, she sipped her coffee and gazed out at the ocean view.

"What's on the agenda today?" Grant asked as he slathered butter on the thick slabs of his French toast.

"Glacier Bay. We should be there just before noon." He nodded, drizzling syrup over the top of his breakfast.

Kate shook salt and pepper over her eggs, and began eating.

"So, what were your impressions of our tablemates last night?" Grant asked. He knew from past experience that she had an excellent insight into people. That's what made her an award-winning journalist and photographer.

She buttered her rye toast, and replied.

"Aiko and Kenji are delightful. Arnold Caldwell, I don't trust at all. Way too smooth. And his wife, Julia? A battered woman...at least, emotionally. Mindy...something odd about her. And Sal? Not at all sure where he fits in."

"Wow, you're amazing," Grant said with a laugh. "You got all that from casual conversation over dinner?"

She looked up at him with a crooked smile.

"Hey, that's what they pay me big bucks for."

"The Napa Register? Somehow, I doubt that."

"Well, I can dream, can't I?"

They finished their breakfasts and returned to their cabin to retrieve jackets. And gloves. This may be August, but they were about to enter into cold waters, surrounded by ice.

Other passengers, similarly dressed, assembled onto the spacious deck at the bow of the ship as it glided silently into Glacier Bay. The sky was overcast, and looming ahead of the ship was a massive glacier. Kate hadn't really known what to expect, but she was surprised to see the jagged towering wall of ice, streaked with lines of brown, indicating layers of dirt deposits, along with crevices of dark blue. The ship moved closer, and the silence was palpable.

Then they heard it...the booming sound of calving. The front edge of the glacier was crumbing, sending huge chunks of ice plunging into the bay, with water spraying upwards. Gasps were heard amongst the passengers, and everyone seemed to have a phone or camera pointing at the display.

Kate took a series of burst photos with her iPhone, then looked down at the icy waters of the bay and took photos of seagulls perched on small chunks of ice.

It was a mesmerizing moment.

Later they withdrew to deck chairs, and were brought mugs of hot chocolate.

"That was an incredible experience," Grant said, gazing back at the bay as the cruise ship slowly reentered the Gulf of Alaska. "I wish I'd studied up on glaciers before we came..." He turned to look at Kate and smirked. "...but somehow I think you did."

She responded with a smirk of her own.

"You should know by now how much I love research," she chuckled. "I learned that although there are lots of different types of glaciers, in this part of Alaska, they are mostly tidewater glaciers, meaning they terminate in the sea. And they're always moving, from the weight of the snow that accumulates each year."

"So, are they coming or going?"

"Both, actually. Most of them locally are currently in retreating cycles."

"I assume they're left over from the last ice age?"

"Correct. They once were part of vast ice sheets like we see now in Antarctica."

"That calving process...I guess that's how icebergs are formed."

"Yes...and those we just saw were puny compared to some. Like the one that sunk the Titanic." Grant looked over the edge of the ship into the innocent-looking floating chunks of ice all around them.

"Puny...but impressive, nonetheless."

After warming their insides with the hot chocolate, they stopped in the deli to eat a light lunch. Kate spotted Aiko and Kenji at a table, and were waved over.

"Please, join us," Aiko said with a smile.

"Thanks, we will," Kate said as she sat down. Grant unloaded their dishes and returned the empty tray to the busing stand before joining them.

Kenji was polishing off some sushi, and Aiko had a brown rice bowl filled with veggies and what looked like marinated chicken.

"What did you think of Glacier Bay?" Kate asked the couple, drizzling dressing on her chef salad.

"I'd seen travel videos, but it doesn't compare to the real thing," Kenji replied.

"Seriously," Kate agreed. "I have friends who have been on this Inside Passage cruise, but even seeing their photos doesn't do it justice. God's creation is simply amazing." She noticed a response to her remark about God in Kenji's eyes.

"You follow Jesus?" the Filipino asked.

"Yes, we do!" Kate was delighted to realize they were apparently with fellow believers.

"Both of our parents are missionaries," Aiko said, "from Korea. Benji and I met in high school on the mission field. We both went away to different colleges, but reconnected via social media a few years' later." She gave her husband a tender smile.

"What took you to the Philippines?" Grant asked before taking a huge bite of his sandwich.

"Two things," Benji replied. "A job offer from the brokerage firm I'm with now, and the opportunity to spread the Gospel among people we had grown to know and love as kids."

"The Lord definitely uses our giftings and life experiences to further His word," Kate agreed.

"And you're on your honeymoon, right?" Aiko asked.

"Yes, we are," Kate replied, giving Grant a warm smile. "And we knew each other in high school as well. But life took us different directions, and like you, we reconnected later."

They continued to chat while they finished their lunches, and parted for the afternoon, saying they would see each other at the formal dinner later than evening.

When Kate emerged from their bathroom after doing her hair and makeup later that day, she found Grant already dressed.

"Hey, I recognize that outfit," she smiled, admiring the jacket and slacks he had worn at their wedding.

"I figured if I looked good enough then for you to marry, it'd be a sure thing for tonight." He eyed her standing in front of him in lacy black underwear. "I supposed you're going to insist on putting that little black dress on, aren't you?"

She blushed and retrieved it from the tiny closet.

"Yes, I am," she said firmly, stepping into it and turning around so he could fasten the back zipper. He complied, but not without planting a soft kiss on the back of her neck.

"Thank you." She reached over to the small table and picked up the jewelry box. "And if you'll do the honors..." She turned to face the mirror.

He lifted the delicate necklace and fastened it around her neck.

"Beautiful."

"It really is," she admitted, putting on the matching earrings and watching the sapphires and diamonds sparkle as she moved.

"Alright, Cinderella, all you need is a pair of shoes and we can go to the ball." She laughed and slipped into her strappy black heels.

"If the Prince is ready, so am I." She picked up a small black clutch purse and took his arm as they exited their cabin. They made their way to the main dining room, and discovered a photographer taking portraits against a lighted backdrop. Grant looked at Kate, questioning her with a raised eyebrow.

"Sure, why not?" she smiled. "We need to commemorate this cruise, and this will be so much nicer than another selfie." She quickly completed the form before stepping beside her new husband and smiling for the camera.

They reached their dining table to find Aiko and Kenji already seated. As they were getting settled into chairs next to the young couple, the Caldwells arrived. He was impeccably dressed in a black suit that she was sure cost more than Grant's monthly salary, and Julia was decked out in a floor length burgundy dress. Mindy and Sal followed them, and Kate tried to get a read on their relationship. Even though Sal pulled out Mindy's chair and seated her, she hardly gave him a glance. Were they a couple? Or just colleagues? Not that it really mattered, but Kate was curious, nonetheless.

"Good evening," Arnold greeted the others as he helped his wife get comfortable. "I trust you all enjoyed seeing Glacier Bay earlier."

"Oh yes," Aiko enthusiastically replied. "Simply amazing." They all chimed in, sharing their impressions.

After ordering drinks and choosing entrees, Arnold Caldwell suddenly stood, pulling his vibrating phone from his pocket.

"Excuse me, I need to take this call." He quickly walked away from the table and out into the hallway. Kate looked over at Julia, who gave a little sigh before taking a sip of her water. Some men could never leave their business behind and enjoy a vacation, and apparently Arnold was such a man.

He returned about five minutes later, appearing elated about something. He paused beside Sal long enough to exchange knowing looks, then returned to his seat between Julia and Grant.

The server brought salads, and baskets of hot rolls. Kate and Aiko were discussing the excursions they each had selected when the ship docked in Skagway the next day. Buttering a roll, Grant turned to Arnold.

"You mentioned last night your company is Caldwell Industries. Are you in manufacturing?"

Arnold swallowed a bite of Caesar salad, and nodded.

"We are a conglomerate, actually, making a wide variety of products including equipment for the fishing and gaming industries to wind and solar generating systems."

"That's interesting. Must have made a few acquisitions along the way," Grant commented. "Where are you based?"

"Our headquarters are in Las Vegas, Nevada." He gave a satisfied smirk. "Definitely a corporate-friendly state." Very friendly, Grant thought, remembering that there was no corporate tax in Nevada. Apparently enough money flowed into the state coffers from the gambling industry to cover budget expenditures.

Over the entrees, Kate tried to engage Julia in conversation, asking about her involvement in the non-profits her husband had mentioned at dinner the previous evening.

"I'm on the board of the hospital auxiliary," she replied. Kate knew the auxiliary was a long way from the image of gray-haired ladies knitting booties and stitching receiving blankets for the maternity ward. These days it was more about raising funds for astronomically expensive medical equipment.

"That sounds challenging...and rewarding, I'm sure."

Julia gave a small smile.

"We just opened a wing dedicated to nuclear medicine, actually. But I have to admit I rather enjoy my involvement with the local arts council." That sounded more interesting to Kate, as well, so she pursued it.

"What kind of things does the council do?" She sat back as the server cleared her dinner plate, and took a sip of her wine.

"We sponsor art classes, and a community theater group. They produce three shows a year, including one musical, and are quite talented. One of our female leads landed a role in an off-Broadway production last year."

"You certainly sound like a busy lady," Kate said admiringly. Julia gave a brief glance at her husband, who was in a deep conversation with Grant.

"Arnie...his business takes a lot of his time, and involves quite a bit of travel. I like to feel useful."

That was a telling remark, thought Kate, and explained what she had observed about the couple. Of course, they had been married, what, thirty years? But somehow Kate couldn't imagine her and Grant being that disconnected at that stage in their marriage. At least, she certainly hoped that wouldn't be the case!

35

CHAPTER EIGHT

The wind was whipping Kate's curls as their rubber raft was carried along the fast-moving Chilkat River through the bald eagle preserve. The river was wide and shallow, shifting throughout the day around areas of rock-strewn sand bars. The guides of the four rafts were obviously well experienced, expertly guiding the vessels that each held six passengers through the channels in the river. The clouds hung low on the mountains, and weathered buildings clung to the shore against pine-covered hills with a backdrop of snow-covered mountains rising steeply behind them.

"Over there," Grant said, gesturing beyond his side of the raft. Kate turned and saw three young bald eagles, evidenced by their speckled brown and white feathers, perched on fallen branches in the middle of the stream. They were staring intently into the churning milky water.

"How on earth can they see anything?" she asked.

"Beats me," Grant replied. Just then, an adult eagle swooped low over the water, talons extended, and rose triumphantly with a wiggling fish clutched in its grasp.

"Shoot, I wish I'd been ready to catch that on video!" Kate cried.

"I think I got a photo at least," Grant replied. "I'll check when we stop for lunch."

Kate gave him a thumbs-up and turned back to her side of the raft. As much as she loved the cruise ship experience, there was something to be said for getting out into God's creation and experiencing it up close and personal. The day had begun after the ship had docked in Skagway, a charming town left from the Klondike gold rush. A high-speed catamaran had taken them to the small town of Haines, where they boarded a motor coach that transported them to the eagle preserve. Donning life vests and rubber boots, they piled into the inflatable rafts and set off down the river.

Even though it was described as *the* place to see bald eagles, they also saw a herd of moose crossing the river, and a black bear watching from shore as they floated past.

At the end of the trip, the rafts were beached on the shore, where a picnic lunch awaited them in a small clearing in the woods. Kate sat on a wooden bench next to Grant and breathed in the intoxicating scents that surrounded them.

"This is heavenly," she sighed. "I'm so glad you suggested this excursion."

"Me too," he agreed, taking a bite of his sandwich. "When's the hike through the rainforest?"

"That's not until Ketchikan, our last port. Tomorrow we go to Juneau..."

"Oh yeah, and Taku Lodge. Definitely looking forward to that!"

They returned to the cruise ship just after 3:00, with enough time for a short nap before cleaning up for dinner. Wearing jeans and sweaters, they were back to casual attire. As they approached the main dining room, Kate pointed to the photos displayed at the entrance.

"Oh look, there we are!" she exclaimed.

"Not bad...we clean up well," Grant chuckled. They perused the photos in their package, electing to take one 8x10 for themselves, a 5x7 for his parents, and a few 4x6s just because.

They were the first to arrive at their table, but he noticed the Caldwells just entering the room. Julia, Mindy and Sal were also dressed more casually, but Arnold wore a sport jacket, albeit without a tie. Grant wondered if he ever wore jeans and a sweatshirt. He doubted it. They guy looked like he expected CNN to show up at any moment.

Aiko and Kenji dashed in just as the server had approached the table to take drink orders. Soon everyone was describing their day in port. Aiko and Kenji had gone ziplining, while the other four had stayed and toured Skagway. Kate passed her iPhone around the table, displaying photos of the eagle preserve.

"What are you all doing tomorrow?" she asked.

"We're doing Mendenhall Glacier, along with visiting the salmon hatchery," Kenji replied. "How about you?"

"Floatplane to Taku Lodge for a salmon bake," Kate replied. Julia's eye lit up.

"So are we! That is, except Arnie. He has a meeting."

A meeting? thought Grant. Probably business...Juneau was the state capital, after all. And he had indicated his company had some involvement with equipment for the fishing industry.

After dinner, Kate excused herself to use the ladies' room before dessert and coffee were to be served. She had just exited a stall and was about to wash her hands when Mindy came in. She glanced around the restroom, appearing a bit nervous. Instead of entering a stall, she walked up next to Kate.

"You said you're a journalist, right?" she asked softly.

"Yes, that's correct." She wondered where this conversation was going.

"Investigative reporting? Or just...neighborhood stuff."

Kate laughed. "Now that I work for the Napa Valley Register, I do end up doing some 'neighborhood stuff.' But when I was in San Francisco, I enjoyed in-depth reporting."

"Well, I was wondering..." she stopped abruptly when the restroom door opened, and Julia came in. Grabbing a paper towel, Mindy wiped off her dry hands, stuffed the crumpled towel into the waste basket and hurried out the door. Kate tried not to stare at the retreating woman, and finished washing her hands. Smiling at Julia, she went back to the table where dessert was just being served.

Mindy avoided eye contact with Kate for the rest of the meal, and dutifully let Sal escort her out of the dining room behind the Caldwells.

"Well, that was strange," Kate murmured as she watched everyone leave.

"What was?" Grant asked, polishing off the last bite of his cheesecake.

She told him about Mindy approaching her in the restroom and her reaction when Julia came in.

"I got the feeling she wanted to tell me something...something confidential."

"Hmmm. Maybe you'll have a chance to talk to her tomorrow, since they're doing the Taku Lodge excursion, too."

"Yeah, we'll see. If we have a chance to talk alone. Anyway, I'm ready to head back to our cabin, what about you?"

"Definitely," he said with a smile spreading across his face.

CHAPTER NINE

The floatplane lifted off the water and soared into the air, circling up and away from Juneau. Soon they were flying over the vast glacier fields, which looked like frozen rivers winding their way through the mountains. The glaciers they saw in Glacier Bay were impressive, but they were truly awe-inspiring from this perspective. The high winged aircraft allowed virtually unobstructed views, and Kate was furiously snapping pictures with her iPhone. Signs of habitation were few and far between, with almost no roads at all between the tiny communities; even driving between major cities was limited. Most transportation was done by boat or plane.

The floatplane began its descent, and Grant pointed to a private marina with small boats tied up to one dock, and a float plane at another. The pilot circled and came in for a smooth landing on Taku River, then slowly taxied to the open spot at the dock.

Kate and Grant were some of the first passengers to deplane. He grabbed her hand and led her up the path towards the lodge. The log building sat at the top of a low rise, with views of Hole-in-the-Wall Glacier across the river.

"This is gorgeous," Kate exclaimed. Her head was on a swivel as they climbed the steps carved into the hillside. The group was met in front of the lodge by a young woman dressed in jeans and a plaid flannel shirt.

"Welcome to Taku Glacier Lodge," she said with a warm smile. "Before we enter the dining room, let me give you a little history of this special place. It was built in 1923 by Dr. Harry DeVighne as one of Alaska's first hunting and fishing lodges open to overnight guests. It was used as a base camp for excursions all around the valleys and streams of the Taku River. It has changed hands over the years, and at one time in the '30s, the owner raised sled dogs here, putting them to work in the winter hauling firewood and using them for travel on the frozen river.

"Today, it is one of the most popular tour destinations in this part of Southeast Alaska, offering a mouth-watering fresh salmon bake." She gestured to her left, to a covered outdoor kitchen at the end of the lodge, where a man was stoking the fire in the stone-walled barbecue.

"This is the real deal," Grant said admiringly, noticing the large stack of split firewood stacked against one wall in the enclosure. "No charcoal briquets here." The man was carefully laying huge slabs of salmon onto a wire basket, then closing the top. Soon the tempting aroma of wood smoked salmon began wafting their direction.

"Now, if you'll follow me..." Their hostess turned and led the way into the dining room. The cozy room held wooden tables with high backed padded chairs. Kerosene lamps and small electric lamps lit the rustic space, and stuffed bears and wolves stared down at them from the log walls. Kate dropped her tote bag on a chair and began admiring photos of the lodge and its visitors from years gone by. Grant retrieved glasses of water from the antique buffet and took them to their table. There were about 18 people in the group, and he noted that Julia Caldwell led Mindy and Sal to a table on the other side of the room.

Everyone sat down, and servers appeared with dishes of coleslaw, baked beans and sourdough bread. Soon the salmon was brought in, resting on wooden platters and placed in the middle of each table. Grant offered to portion out the salmon, and within minutes everyone's plates were piled high. Kate discovered that two of the couples at their table were from another cruise ship, and discussion was lively over the meal.

Just as Grant was professing that he was beyond full, the servers appeared with hot Russian tea and ginger cookies.

"Oh my...can't pass those up!" he groaned as he helped himself to two warm cookies.

Their hostess, whom they had learned was Laura, stood and got their attention.

"Now you have free time to enjoy as you like; we offer a guided nature walk, or you may choose to just wander the many trails yourselves. Or you may decide to sit in the warm sun and enjoy the beauty of your surroundings. Just remember to keep your eyes out for black bears – they can't resist the aroma of fresh grilled salmon either! We also have a gift shop in the building next door with items to remember your Taku Lodge adventure, so be sure to stop in before you leave."

"So, what do you think?" Kate asked as they pushed back their chairs and stood.

"Since a nap probably isn't an option, how about we check out those trails she mentioned?"

"Good choice. I'm going to stop in the restroom first, so I'll meet you out front."

By the time she rejoined Grant, everybody else had scattered. One couple was taking selfies in front of the carved black bear, and others were walking down to the water.

"There are trail markers over there," Grant said, pointing behind the barbecue pavilion. He reached out and took her hand, and they walked over the thick green grass to the edge of the woods. A tall pole held four signs, pointing in various directions.

"Taku falls, 1.2 miles," Kate read. "I like the sound of that one." Grant nodded in agreement, and they set off. The path wound through the verdant, old-growth forest. Colorful flowers and toadstools caught Kate's photographic eye, and she frequently paused to capture them with her camera. After walking for several minutes, they could hear the distinct sounds of falling water.

"We must be close to the falls," she commented. But then a piercing cry broke through the peaceful setting.

"What was that?" she asked, grabbing Grant's sleeve to stop him.

"Not sure; I supposed it could be a wounded animal," he replied. She shook her head emphatically.

"No, that was no rabbit. It sounded human. Come on!" She dashed off up the path, trying to determine the direction the cry had been coming from. Rounding a bend, they came to a wall of rock, with the waterfall coursing down it. She stopped, turning in a circle.

"I don't see anything..." she started to say. Just then, she caught sight of something yellow off the path to the right. "Over there." She pushed through the branches to see what it was, when they heard something crashing through the underbrush. Grant was on her heels and came to a sudden stop beside her.

"It looks like somebody's been hurt," he said. The figure, a woman judging by the long auburn hair, was lying face down, right arm stretched out. Grant knelt down in the wet leaves and felt for a pulse.

Nothing.

He gently rolled her over.

Kate gasped. It was Mindy.

And long bloody gashes scarred her face and neck.

CHAPTER TEN

Lieutenant Davis snapped his notebook closed and tucked it in his shirt pocket. The State Trooper looked over his shoulder where the forensic team was completing their inspection of the body.

"We'll have to wait for the autopsy, but it appears to be a bear attack that killed your friend." Kate blanched.

"Does that...is that common?" she finally asked.

"Rare, but it has happened," the slender officer responded. "According to the workers at the lodge, they have seen a mother black bear with two cubs in the area. It's possible Ms. Marshall surprised them."

Kate hugged her arms tightly around her and shivered.

"Have you talked to Mrs. Caldwell?" she asked. "Mindy worked for her husband, and she and Julia were on the excursion together."

"My partner has taken her statement. Apparently, Mrs. Caldwell didn't feel like hiking the trails, and went to the gift shop instead."

"So, Mindy was walking by herself..." Grant concluded.

"That's how it appears. Another guest saw her walk into the forest not too long before you two did."

"But what about Sal?" Kate interjected. "He and Mindy seemed to be a couple."

"None of the witnesses so far have mentioned him. But he was seen a few minutes ago with Mrs. Caldwell. I'll be sure to follow up to determine his whereabouts a half hour ago."

"What happens now?" Before the Trooper could answer, one of the forensic team members approached, ripping off his vinyl gloves.

"Excuse me," the middle-aged man interrupted. "But this may not have been a bear attack after all." All eyes were suddenly upon him, waiting for him to explain. "The scratch marks don't fit the pattern of a bear paw, and there are no bite marks at all. And no evidence that she was being dragged into the forest."

"But...but we heard the bear crashing through the woods," Kate protested. "We must have scared it away."

"You undoubtedly heard *something*," he replied firmly, "but it wasn't a bear. A mother bear would definitely not have been scared away that easily from a food source when she's feeding two little ones." *A food source.* Kate's stomach lurched at that remark.

Lieutenant Davis frowned and turned back to Grant and Kate.

"Well, this definitely changes things. If this is indeed a homicide, we'll have to ask you to stay until the Alaska Bureau of Investigation can be brought in."

Kate was aghast. "But we're on a cruise...on our honeymoon..."

"I understand, and I'm sorry to have to detain you. One of my Troopers will accompany you back to the ship where you can gather your things. We'll put you up in a hotel in Juneau."

Kate turned to look at Grant, and he simply shrugged his shoulders. He knew all too well about procedures in an investigation of this nature.

"Will the Caldwells and Mr. Dimarco be asked to stay in Juneau as well?"

"Yes, they will." He turned to the forensic investigator. "Thanks, Hal...if there's nothing else you need me for, I'll escort the Thompsons back to the lodge."

Grant put his arm around Kate's shoulders as they walked away from the grisly scene in the woods. Kate's thoughts were swirling. Mindy had wanted to talk to her last night in the restroom on the cruise ship, but had been interrupted by Julia. What had she wanted to tell her?

Now Kate would never know.

* * *

"Thanks, Clark, I'll keep you posted." Grant disconnected the call and tossed his cell phone on the bed. Kate was unpacking their hastily gathered belongings and putting them away in the hotel room.

"At least they put us up in this quaint hotel," she said, hanging Grant's suit and her dress into the antique wardrobe. Over 100 years old, it was one of the first hotels in the frontier mining camp that Juneau had once been. The restored late Victorian building retained its Queen Anne charm, which Kate much preferred over the typical sterile hotel chain.

"And it has a much-heralded bar," he added. "I suggest we head downstairs and sample a local brew." Kate closed the doors to the wardrobe and turned to smile at her new husband.

"Lead the way, dear."

He closed and locked their room door with the old-fashioned key and they walked down the wood-plank hallway with oriental style runners to the stairway. They descended to the first floor, and crossed the lobby to the bar and restaurant.

"Oh my," Kate exclaimed as they entered. Hanging baskets of wisteria graced the replica Tiffany stained glass windows facing the street. An old upright piano was on one side of a seating area, comprised of antique furniture. The heavily carved bar ran along the back of the room, where most of the stools were already occupied.

"Let's sit by the window," Kate suggested. Grant nodded and walked over to a loveseat with a view of both the street and the bar. A waitress approached, and Grant asked for her recommendation of the best local beer. Kate deferred, asking for a glass of Merlot. The young woman was back in a flash, also putting a dish of mixed nuts on the table in front of them. Grant took an exploratory sip of the foaming brew, and nodded with a smile. The waitress set down a menu 'just in case' and left. Kate let out a deep sigh.

"Not the way I expected our day to end, to say the least."

"Definitely not," he agreed, stretching his arm across the back of the loveseat and squeezing her shoulder.

"Poor Mindy...I wonder what happened?"

"We'll know for sure after the autopsy. Lieutenant Davis said her body would be flown to Anchorage, where the State Medical Examiner's office is located. There's a satellite office of the ABI here in Juneau, so I imagine we'll be hearing from them tomorrow."

Just then Arnold Caldwell entered without glancing in their direction, and walked over to greet a man dressed in a business suit who was seated at the bar. After ordering a draft beer, he sat down next to the man and they were soon deep in a discussion. After a couple of minutes, he pulled out his cell phone, scrolled down the screen, and handed the phone to his companion to look at.

"That's interesting," Grant said. "I wonder if that's who Caldwell was having the business meeting with today?"

"For someone whose assistant was possibly murdered today, he doesn't seem too distressed," Kate said dryly.

"And I wonder where Sal is?" Grant continued.

"They all must be staying here as well," Kate mused. "Maybe he's with Julia. I doubt she's taking the situation quite as coolly as her husband appears to be."

Grant looked thoughtful. "What's your sense of the relationship between Mindy and Sal?"

Kate sighed and slowly shook her head. "Not sure. He seemed to act like they were a couple, but I didn't get that feeling from her. And she *was* about to tell me something last night...if only Julia hadn't come in the restroom at that very moment!"

"I'd like to find out more about Caldwell Industries," Grant said. "If Mindy was in fact murdered, I'm wondering if it's tied to the company in some way."

"I really thought our honeymoon wouldn't include a murder investigation, but I guess I was wrong!"

CHAPTER ELEVEN

Grant and Kate were finishing breakfast the following morning when his phone buzzed.

"This is Grant. Oh, hello Lieutenant...thank you, we'll be expecting him." He disconnected the call and took a last sip of coffee. "The agent from the Alaska Bureau of Investigation is on his way. He'll meet us in the lobby."

A few minutes later, a tall lanky man wearing a suit and carrying a small briefcase strode into the lobby. His visual sweep landed on the couple sitting next to a potted palm and he approached them.

"Mr. and Mrs. Thompson?" Grant stood and shook his outstretched hand.

"Yes. Please join us."

"Thank you," he said, sitting down in a facing chair. "Agent Adam Wilcox, with the ABI." If Grant had to guess, he'd say the agent was probably in his early 40s, with a closely cropped beard. He pulled his cell phone out of his pocket and placed it on the trunk that served as a coffee table between them.

"If you don't mind, I'd like to record this conversation. Much more accurate than trying to scribble some notes." Grant smiled and nodded in agreement. "I understand you and your wife are from Napa, California, where you are the County Sheriff." The man had obviously done his homework.

"That's correct. Kate and I are on a Princess cruise for our honeymoon." Agent Wilcox turned to address Kate.

"And I understand you are a journalist for the Napa Valley Register, correct?"

She started to nod a reply, then remembered the recording. "Yes, I am."

"Prior to that, you were employed by the San Francisco Chronicle as a photojournalist, where you were nominated for a Pulitzer Prize for a piece on neighborhood rioting during the pandemic." Kate's eyes widened.

"Yes...yes, that's true. I returned home to Napa to take care of my mother during the last few months of her life."

Agent Wilcox paused and smiled.

"As it happens, my wife and I vacationed in Napa Valley two years ago and read about you two being instrumental in solving the murder of the gossip columnist, Monica Farnsworth."

Grant shook his head, chuckling.

"I guess the old saying about it being a small world is accurate."

"Indeed. But more importantly, I'm hoping you will be able to assist in this matter as well."

"We'll be happy to answer any questions you may have," Grant replied.

"Actually, I'm hoping you are willing to help more than just providing a few observations. The ABI is stretched thin right now, partly because we have such a large territory to cover, but also due to recent threats of sabotage against the Trans-Alaska Pipeline. Since you are a member of law enforcement, I'd like to authorize you to assist in this investigation. That is, if you're willing."

Grant glanced at Kate, whose expression was benign. But he thought he detected the hint of a smile. Knowing her, she was probably already mentally rubbing her hands together in anticipation of another mystery to solve. He cleared his throat, and looked back at the agent.

"Assuming our employers don't object, I would be happy to assist the ABI."

Agent Wilcox broke into a wide smile.

"Wonderful! Now then, let's cover what you've witnessed so far regarding Mindy Marshall's death."

They spent close to an hour going over what they had observed, from the first meeting over dinner on the cruise ship to the present day. Kate also explained the brief encounter with Mindy in the ladies' room that seemed to indicate the young woman had intended to share something confidential with her.

"As you can well imagine, Agent Wilcox," Kate said, "I love doing research. Which can be very time-consuming, I know. If I can help in that regard, please let me know."

"I was hoping you'd offer, Kate. We need to do a deep dive on the Caldwells, both personally and professionally. And Sal Dimarco as well. I'm sure as a journalist you have resources, but I can offer access to ones that are beyond your purview. Let me send you contact info on Pamela Russell. She is an analyst at the Bureau, and a whiz at unearthing information. I'll send you my contact information, too."

They all pulled out their phones to share their data. After the ABI agent left, with plans to reconvene the next morning, Grant and Kate went up to their room to begin their assignments. This was turning into a working honeymoon.

First things first, Grant called Clark, the Chief Deputy Sheriff, and gave him a heads-up. And Kate put in a call to her editor at the Register, Dan Griffith.

"You're turning into a murder magnate," he said with a chuckle when she told him what had transpired. "But knowing you two, you'll sort it out in no time. And I'm sure the news wires will pick this up once we start publishing details. Keep me posted!"

"I'm not sure I like being called a 'murder magnate,' actually," Kate mumbled after ending the call.

"Is that what Dan said?" Grant said, trying not to laugh, as he plugged in his laptop. "You are really good at what you do, you know. He's just putting a bit of a spin on it."

"Humph. I guess." She also set up her laptop, thankful that she'd brought it with her. Kate decided to do some basic searches using the tools she had before she resorted to contacting the ABI analyst. No sense covering the same territory twice.

"Agent Wilcox wants me to do preliminary interviews with the Caldwells and Sal. I'd appreciate you being there, too. I think it will be less threatening to them that way, and I know you'll pick up on things I'd miss."

"Okay, when are you thinking?"

"This afternoon. Ideally, we'll talk to each of them individually. You get started on your research, and I'll put together a timeline of events."

Kate began with standard searches on everyone involved, including social media accounts. She quickly found basic information on each of them, including addresses for the past several years.

When their stomachs sent up warnings, Grant ordered room service for lunch. While they ate, Grant suggested they recap what they had so far.

Grant had put together a spread sheet with everything he knew about all four individuals since arriving on the cruise ship, including cabin numbers. He had contacted the ship bursar, and requested time stamped receipts for venues and shops to correlate with the various events.

Then it was Kate's turn.

"I started with Mindy. She was 25, single, and had worked for Caldwell Industries since she graduated from UNLV, where she majored in business management and minored in accounting.

She owns a modest condo in Henderson, and belongs to a gym where she works out an average of three days a week. She shops at Safeway, and places numerous orders on Amazon each month. She attended a non-denominational fellowship where she participated in a singles group. Her social media accounts show her mostly with family; parents, one older brother, and his two children. I did see a photo she was tagged in from a company party, and she was standing next to Sal and drinking a glass of wine."

"Wow, that's impressive!"

"Thanks. I plan to contact the data analyst at ABI for help in accessing bank accounts and phone records."

"Any court records found for her?"

"No, other than the Warranty Deed when she purchased her condo two years ago. Conventional mortgage, so she must have had a sizeable down-payment."

"Really? That's interesting for a... what, she would have been 23 at the time?"

"That's what I thought, too. Could be family money, of course. It will take more digging to find that out."

"Anything else on our victim?"

"No, that's it for the moment. I researched Julia next. Age 55, a graduate from Vassar. They were married as reported, 30 years ago. No children that I could find. Verified her participation in the hospital auxiliary. There are several media releases showing her at the dedication of the nuclear medicine wing. Her social media has photos advertising classes at the art center, and posters for upcoming theater events."

"No red flags, apparently." Grant stood and stretched, walking to the window that overlooked the street two stories below.

"Not yet, anyway. Again, we need to check out bank accounts and phone records." She tapped her pencil on the table.

"Salvatore Dimarco, however, is a different story. He didn't exist five years ago."

Grant whipped around and looked at her with raised eyebrows.

"Seriously? You didn't find anything for him?"

"No, I didn't say that. I said I can't find anything dating before 2018. According to his driver's license, which was issued that year, he's 27 years old and lives in a condo."

"Let me guess. Same complex where Mindy lives?"

"Different unit, but yes. It's owned by a corporation – Diamond Investments. It will take some time to run that down."

Grant rubbed the back of his neck as he paced in front of the window.

"Were you able to find out anything else about him?"

"No social media accounts that I could find."

"Hmmm...hopefully the bursar has some receipts from purchases he's made on the ship. Otherwise, looks like we'll need help from the ABI on him, too."

"And last, but definitely not least, Arnold Edward Caldwell. 57 years old, grew up in New York City – the Bronx, specifically – and attended City College. It doesn't seem that he graduated, though. He has quite a presence online – same smile in almost all the photos. He formed Caldwell Industries 28 years ago, and from its start in a somewhat rundown neighborhood, they moved up to a modern high-rise where they occupy the top floor. The Caldwells live in the Las Vegas bedroom community of Henderson, in a 6,500 square foot home with pool and tennis court."

"Not too shabby for a kid from the hood," Grant commented dryly.

"Seriously. I'll start digging into Caldwell Industries and try to peel back the layers that I'm sure exist."

Grant glanced at his watch. "That will have to wait, I'm afraid. Time to visit with the Caldwells." Not wanting to seem too intimidating, Grant left his laptop in their room, bringing only a small notebook. They took the stairs down to the second floor, and found room 211. Julia opened the door within moments of Grant's knock. Dressed in jeans and a sweatshirt emblazoned with the Princess Cruise Line logo, she invited them in. Kate couldn't help but notice that the usually impeccable socialite seemed a tad frazzled. Her hair looked as though she'd just gotten up from a nap, and her mascara was smudged. She removed a room service tray, which Kate noticed appeared to be a meal for one, and set it outside in the hallway before closing the door.

"Is your husband here?" Grant asked.

"No, he...he had a meeting, and said he'd be back as soon as he could." She glanced around the small room.

"Shall we sit here?" she suggested, gesturing at the small table with four chairs. Grant nodded, and they all sat down in front of the window which framed a backdrop of snow-capped mountains.

"As you probably already know, I've been asked to help the Alaska Bureau of Investigation gather some information to help them in their investigation of Mindy's death." Julia bit her lower lip and nodded. Grant took out his notebook and pen and held them in his lap.

"Tell me a little bit about Mindy. How long had she worked for your husband?"

"About...three years, I think. She was fresh out of college. His former secretary, Norma, had been with him for almost twenty years, and was retiring."

"Norma must have been like his right arm," Grant commented. "It must have been hard to see her go."

"Oh yes, it definitely was. Arnie was beside himself. He probably interviewed a dozen women before he finally hired Mindy."

"After someone with Norma's background, were you surprised that he hired someone with virtually no work experience?" Kate asked.

Julia let out a sigh. "Yes, a bit...although she was highly recommended by the university."

"What were her responsibilities?" Grant asked, jotting a couple of notes while he talked.

"Well...you'll have to ask Arnie, but I think she basically coordinated his calendar. You know, scheduling appointments, meetings, that kind of thing. And she also worked with the accounting department. Arnie has a thing about knowing all the numbers from each of the subsidiaries..."

"What about company events?" He asked. "Did she help plan and host those?"

"Yes, she did. She apparently was very detail-oriented, which Arnie appreciated."

"What can you tell us about her personal life?" Kate asked. "Was she dating anyone?"

Julia shrugged her shoulders before responding. "Not really, unless you can count Sal." Kate and Grant exchanged a quick look then waited for Julia to continue. "I think she broke off a relationship a year or so ago. Somebody she knew at college."

Kate spoke again. "So, she's been seeing Sal, then?"

"I think so. At least, I've seen them together at company functions. I was a bit surprised he came along on the cruise, actually."

"What is Sal's job at Caldwell Industries?" Kate asked. Julia hesitated and gave a small shrug.

"I don't know his actual title," she said, her gaze wandering to the view out the window. "But Arnie seems to include him in meetings and press conferences...things like that. So maybe he's like a press secretary?"

Grant didn't think Julia sounded very confident about that, and made a note to follow up with both Arnold and Sal.

They spent the next several minutes verifying details about her charitable involvements, and typical daily routine. Then Kate switched gears.

"What made you decide on an Alaska cruise to celebrate your 30th wedding anniversary?" Julia looked down at her hands before responding.

"It was Arnie's idea, actually. He came home one evening and told me he'd already made the reservations for the cruise."

That struck Kate as interesting.

"What about previous vacations? Was he usually the decision-maker?" Now Julia was really looking uncomfortable.

"We...Arnie travels so much with his business, that he doesn't..." Grant noticed she was literally wringing a tissue she had been holding. "This is the first real vacation we've had in...years." He brought the conversation back to the events at Taku Glacier Lodge.

"What can you tell us about the excursion to the lodge? What did you all do after lunch?"

"Mindy wanted to explore the trails, but I wasn't really up for a hike. So, I decided to go to the gift shop."

"What about Sal?" Kate asked

"The last I saw him, he was ordering a beer at the small bar in the dining room. I was looking through sweatshirts in the gift shop when I heard a lot of commotion and shouting from outside. When I went out front, one of the people from the lodge said there had been a bear attack in the woods, and ushered all of the guests back into the dining room."

"Did you see Sal there?" Julia's eyes narrowed as she tried to remember the scene.

"Yes...he came in just after I did."

"So he had been outside? Grant asked. "He wasn't still in the dining room drinking his beer?"

"No...no, I don't think so. But everything was so confusing, I'm not really sure." She looked distressed, and wadded up the tissue. "A few minutes later, a State Trooper came in and found me. He told me Mindy had been killed, and that those in our group would have to stay in Juneau during the investigation and couldn't rejoin the cruise."

"Did you call your husband?"

"Yes, but I got his voicemail, so I had to leave a message."

Grant had no more questions for Julia, and gave Kate a questioning look in case she did. When she responded with a quick shake of her head, he stood up.

"Thank you, Julia, we appreciate your taking time to talk with us. When your husband returns, please have him call me so we can speak with him as well." Grant handed her one of his Napa County Sheriff's cards as they all moved toward the door. "Do you know if Sal was with him today?" She shook her head apologetically.

"No, I'm sorry, I don't."

"No worries." He and Kate exited the room, and were silent as they went back up to their hotel room. They had no more than shut their door before Kate kicked off her shoes and flopped on the bed.

"Wow...that certainly was interesting." He joined her on the bed, and faced her with his head propped on one hand.

"First impressions?"

"Marriage of convenience. He has his life, she has hers. And she's obviously blissfully ignorant of his business."

"Agreed. And the fact that they've virtually never taken a vacation together in thirty years of marriage..."

"Makes me wonder why now," Kate said thoughtfully.

CHAPTER TWELVE

Grant was beginning to wonder what happened to Arnold Caldwell when his phone rang. He glanced at the screen before he answered. "It's Arnold," he told Kate, who was transcribing their individual notes on the interview with Julia. He pushed the speaker button so she could hear the conversation.

"I understand you'd like to talk to me regarding the unfortunate incident at Taku Lodge." *Unfortunate incident?* Kate thought that was a bit of an understatement. His assistant had been brutally murdered less than 24 hours before, and he was referring to it as an unfortunate incident? Grant apparently shared her reaction, because he raised his eyebrows as he listened.

"Yes, that's correct. The ABI has asked me to assist, and I was hoping to meet with you this afternoon."

"I'm just returning to the hotel. Shall we meet in the Klondike Bar in say, ten minutes?"

"That works for us. We'll meet you there." He disconnected and replaced the phone in his pocket. "Sure doesn't seem too upset about Mindy," he said dryly.

"Mr. Cool," Kate agreed. "He'd make a good politician."

Since it was just after 4:00, few people were in the bar when Grant and Kate arrived. They seated themselves underneath the wisteria at the front window again for privacy. A minute or two later, Arnold Caldwell entered and spotted them. He joined them, sitting in an antique Morris chair. A waitress approached, and Arnie glanced at Kate and Grant.

"It's on me," he said, before ordering a draft beer.

"Sparkling water with lime for us," Kate said. After the waitress left, Arnold addressed Grant.

"Appears you're on a bit of a busman's holiday," he said, loosening his tie.

Grant smiled. "Fortunately, I enjoy what I do. But I'm sure my bride didn't expect my work to invade our honeymoon."

She laughed and shrugged. "As a journalist, I'm never really on vacation, either."

The waitress brought their drinks, and Grant took out his notebook and pen while they waited to be served.

"All right, let's get to it. Arnie, you've indicated you and Julia are taking the cruise to celebrate your 30th anniversary." Arnie took a sip of his beer and nodded. "Who came up with the destination?"

"Mutual decision, actually. She thought a cruise would be relaxing, and I had Mindy check out several options. The Inland Passage seemed a good choice." Kate hoped Grant was making note of the slightly different explanation from Julia's.

"But you missed the excursion yesterday; Julia mentioned at dinner the night before you had a meeting." He let the statement hang, and watched Arnie's body language. He crossed his legs at the knee and popped a few nuts into his mouth before answering.

"Caldwell Industries makes products for the fishing industry, and this seemed a perfect time to make calls on potential clients in the salmon farming business."

"Farm raised salmon? I didn't know they allowed that here," Kate said in surprise.

"It's a bit of a hybrid process," Arnie replied. "The harvest of wild-caught salmon is inherently volatile. So nowadays, much of the salmon is farm raised and then released into the Pacific and rivers locally."

"And you were meeting with clients here in Juneau?" Grant asked. Arnie nodded. "The ABI will want specifics; names, locations, that sort of thing. You can email the info to me." He handed Arnie his card. "Did Sal go with you?"

"No, Sal wanted to go with Mindy and Julia to the lodge." Grant made notes before continuing.

"Let's talk about Mindy. I understand you hired her right out of college?"

"My secretary Norma was retiring after almost twenty years. She knew my operation like she knew her own kitchen. I didn't want to hire someone with years of experience that I would have to retrain to my ways of doing things. That's why I went to the business school at UNLV and had them recommend graduating candidates."

"What exactly did she do for you?" Kate asked.

"At the beginning, the usual secretarial duties. But she was a quick learner, and I began giving her more and more responsibilities. She organized company events, screened potential clients for our various divisions, and worked with the accounting department. I run a tight ship, and need up-to-date facts and figures at the drop of a hat. She's...she *was*...quite good at that."

"And her personal life?" Kate continued.

"Never brought it to work. Although I think Sal was interested in her."

"Let's talk about Sal," Grant said. "What is his position with your company?"

Arnie shifted in the chair, his gaze darting out the window.

"Part chauffer, part sounding board." *And part bodyguard*, Kate surmised. The man was big and beefy, with a no-nonsense attitude.

61

"How long has he been with you?" Kate asked.

"A little over four years," Arnie responded.

"And what did he do before joining Caldwell Industries?" Kate was recalling the absence of data prior to 2018 in her online searches.

"We grew up in the same neighborhood in the Bronx. I knew his father, and he asked me to find his kid a spot in my organization. Was glad to help."

"Was he with you today?"

"Only for my first meeting this morning. I haven't seen him since then."

"Can you think of anyone who would want to harm Mindy?" Grant asked point-blank. Arnie looked surprised and his eyes jumped back and forth between Grant and Kate.

"Harm her? But I thought...it was a bear attack, right?"

"That's questionable. We're waiting on autopsy results to confirm cause of death."

This was the first time Kate had ever seen Arnie look nervous. His normal air of confidence was gone.

They finished the interview a few minutes later, and Kate and Grant remained in the bar after Arnold paid the tab and left. Kate excused herself and went to the ladies' room, and when she returned, found two glasses of wine sitting on the trunk in front of the loveseat. Grant was on his phone, apparently leaving a voice mail.

"Please call me as soon as you receive this message." He rattled off his number and disconnected. "Sal doesn't answer," he remarked, picking up his wine glass. "I'll try him after dinner."

"We can always knock on his door," Kate suggested.

"Yes, it might come to that," he agreed.

"What are you thinking?" Kate asked, taking a sip of her wine.

"After dinner, let's compile our latest notes. But at the moment, I just want to enjoy the next couple of hours with my bride."

CHAPTER THIRTEEN

"That was simply delicious," Kate said with a sigh as the waiter cleared their plates. "I thought we had fresh fish in California, but this..." For once, she was at a loss for words.

"I agree," Grant said, signing their room number on the dinner check. "Ready?"

She smiled and rose from her chair, flicking sourdough breadcrumbs off her jeans. Sal had returned Grant's call during their meal, and agreed to meet with them at 7:00 in his room.

They climbed the stairs to the second floor, and found room 217, across the hall from the Caldwell's. As they passed, Kate could hear the faint sounds of voices from inside their room.

Grant knocked on Sal's door, and exchanged an expectant look with Kate while they waited. The sounds of the TV abruptly stopped, then Sal opened the door and greeted them. He was wearing an untucked flannel shirt over jeans, and heavy socks but no shoes. He obviously liked to work out, evidenced by the shirt sleeves stretched tightly over his biceps.

"Come on in," he said, stepping back so they could pass. The coffee table in front of the TV held the remains of a pizza in its box, and two empty beer bottles. "Can I get you anything?" he asked as he crossed to the small refrigerator.

"No thanks, we're good," Grant replied. "Just finished dinner downstairs."

Sal nodded, retrieving another bottle of beer and twisting off the cap before joining them. He plunked down on the small couch, and Kate and Grant sat in the club chairs.

Grant went into his spiel about helping the Alaska Bureau of Investigation gather background information in Mindy's death.

"How long have you worked for Caldwell Industries?" Grant led off with basic details, flipping to a blank page in his notebook.

Sal took a long pull on the beer before answering.

"Started about four years ago." It didn't appear he was going to elaborate, so Grant kept going.

"And what do you do for them?"

Sal shrugged. "Whatever Mr. Caldwell wants."

"Such as?" Grant wasn't going to let him off with non-answers.

"Drive him places... he says he hates driving in traffic and it's a waste of his time, but more likely it's because he likes to look cool stepping out of the limo." Kate bit her lip to hide a smile that tried to surface. Arnold definitely had the politician persona. Or maybe considering where they lived, that of a celebrity.

"Anything else?"

"Yeah, he likes to run ideas by me. See what I think." Kate thought that was a stretch. A twenty-something kid from the Bronx advising the head of a conglomerate on business decisions? Apparently, Grant had similar thoughts.

"Do you have a business degree?"

"Nah, nothin' like that," he said with a slight snort. "Just street smarts."

"Then how did you come to work for Mr. Caldwell?"

"My dad put in a good word for me. They knew each other from the Bronx."

Grant was scribbling notes as he listened. "What were you doing before you went to work for Caldwell Industries?" Sal squirmed a bit, and finished off the beer in one swallow.

"Odd jobs, mostly. Hadn't found anything I'd consider spending the next thirty years doing."

Kate decided to throw a curve ball. "Were you dating Mindy?" Sal raked his hand through his dark hair and shrugged.

"If you could call it that. We went to company events together, and out to dinner a couple of times. But I think she still had a flame burning for some guy she knew in college. Football jock – quarterback, I think she said. One night when she'd had a bit more wine than usual, she mentioned he had broken it off right after they graduated."

"What kinds of things did she like to do?" Kate asked. "Any hobbies?" He took a deep breath and stared at the ceiling.

"Well...we live in the same condo complex, and one time when I was at her place I saw this contraption in the dining room. She was making a quilt." He set down his empty beer bottle and looked wistfully toward the mini fridge. "And I think she was into genealogy. She mentioned trying to find her birth parents."

Kate perked up hearing this new information.

"Then Mindy was adopted?" she asked.

"Guess so," Sal responded. "She only mentioned it once."

Kate thought back to the night Mindy had approached her in the ladies' room on the ship. Was she going to ask Kate to help her search for her birth parents?

"Give me a rundown of your day yesterday," Grant said.

This time Sal did get up and get another bottle of beer. Grant couldn't help but wonder if he was stalling. He walked to the window and took a sip before turning back to them and answering.

"Had a quick breakfast, then Julia, Mindy and I boarded the floatplane, along with you."

"When did Mr. Caldwell leave?" Grant interjected.

"Not really sure. He was still eating breakfast when we left the cafeteria."

"And after lunch at the lodge?"

"Mindy wanted to check out the trails, but Julia wasn't up for it, so she went over to the gift shop. I got another beer and hung around the lodge. Wandered down to the river...that's about it."

"So, you didn't see Mindy again that afternoon? Didn't follow her into the woods?" Grant was watching Sal's body language closely. He shifted on his feet, shook his head, and crossed his arms across his chest.

"Nope...like I said, I was just hanging out around the lodge."

Kate spoke up. "When did you become aware of what happened to Mindy?"

"I was down by that bench at the river, and heard somebody yelling about a bear attack. That got me moving, and I hurried back up to the lodge. They were rounding everybody up and telling them to go back into the dining room."

"Did you see Julia?"

"Yeah, she was already in there when I went in."

"Who did Arnold meet with this morning?" Sal looked surprised at the quick change in topics.

"Uh...some guy with Fish and Game, I think."

"You think? Didn't you go with him?" Sal opened his mouth, then shut it again. He walked over to the couch and set his beer down on the table before sitting down again.

"Yeah, yeah, I was with him...but I didn't actually go into the guy's office with Arnie. I just waited for him."

"Then what?"

"He said he had some errands to run, that he'd meet me back at the hotel later."

"And what did you do?"

"Nothing, really. Just wandered around, looked into a couple of shops. Had a burger at a little hole-in-the wall. Came back and took a nap."

And undoubtedly stopped for a beer or two, Kate thought. Grant gave Sal a penetrating look.

"Do you have any idea who would want to harm Mindy?"

Sal swallowed, and fought to hold Grant's gaze.

"Nope, I sure don't."

Back in their room, Grant and Kate sat down to compile their notes while the conversations were still fresh in their minds.

"I wish I had a whiteboard," Grant lamented. "I like being able to visualize all the characters involved, and the timeline. And listing possible motives."

"Guess we'll have to do it old-school," Kate said. "I got some copy paper, markers and a tape dispenser from the hotel office." She took down a photo of Juneau in the late 1800s and began taping up sheets of paper on the wall. Grant laughed and planted a kiss on her cheek. Grabbing a marker, he began by listing each person on their own sheet of paper. He placed Mindy, their focus, in the middle, surrounded by the other major players. Underneath each name, he listed their age, relationship to Mindy, and to each other. In the next level out, he showed secondary characters – Sal's father and friend to Arnie, Mindy's ex-boyfriend, and even her unknown birth parents.

In a new grouping, Grant listed a timeline, beginning with the earliest known relevant event: Mindy's graduation from college, Sal's joining Caldwell Industries, and finally the sailing of the cruise ship through the current day.

"I'm going to omit Aiko and Kenji, because not only were they randomly assigned to our dinner table, they weren't on any of the same excursions that any of us took."

"That's fine, but I do see something that's missing." He turned to look at his wife, and she walked up to the wall and tapped Wednesday. "That's the day the ship was in Skagway, and you and I did the eagle preserve, but we don't know what the others did. At least I don't remember them talking about it." He clapped her on the shoulder.

"You're right! It may not be at all important, but we won't know unless we ask." He pulled out his phone and dialed Arnold's number.

"Hello, Mr. Caldwell, sorry to disturb your evening. But I wanted to ask what you and the rest of your party did Wednesday, the day the ship was in port at Skagway?" He had pushed the speaker button so Kate could hear the reply.

"No problem, Grant. We all went on the trip by rail to the...what was it, Julia?" They heard her response in the background.

"White Pass summit."

"Yes, that was it. Next we crossed the river on this suspension bridge...for a tough guy, I wasn't sure Sal would make it across."

"So, all four of you went on the excursion?"

"Yes. We took a tour bus through some beautiful country – saw lots of wildlife – and ended up at a family farm. Quite a long day."

Grant thanked him again and disconnected. Kate was already filling in the information on their timeline.

"Nothing out of the ordinary, it seems," she commented. "In fact, so far we haven't heard any really conflicting information from any of them."

"No, and that's what's so frustrating," Grant agreed, crossing his arms and staring at the wall. "Hard to come up with a motive with what we've got so far."

She looked at Grant. "Maybe it wasn't murder at all..."

As if on cue, Grant's phone dinged, indicating an incoming text.

"It's from Agent Wilcox. The ME completed the autopsy, and cause of death was confirmed to be from a broken hyoid...definitely not a bear attack."

CHAPTER FOURTEEN

With the confirmation that Mindy was indeed murdered, Kate and Grant arose the next morning with renewed resolve. They ordered room service, and ate their omelets while scouring the papers taped to the wall. Grant stood with a mug of hot coffee in his hands, eying the blank paper entitled 'Motive.'

"This is going to be pure speculation, until we have something of substance. Phone records... bank statements... something more concrete."

Kate joined him, and slipped her arm around his waist.

"One thing we could do while we wait for that information is to look at Mindy's belongings. I assume the ABI or the State Troopers have them?"

"Good idea, wife. I'll give Agent Wilcox a call. It may be Saturday, but I doubt he's out fishing."

The ABI agent was indeed at his desk, and confirmed that the contents of Mindy's cabin were still in the ABI Juneau office, pending transfer to the Major Crimes Unit in Anchorage. Grant wrote down the address and said they would be there shortly.

Adam Wilcox met the Thompsons at the front desk of the Bureau and escorted them through security and down a long hall to the Evidence Room.

"I had a chance to read the email summary you sent me last night of the interviews. Very thorough, and I agree that there are no red flags evident."

"When do you think phone records and financial records will be available?" Grant asked.

"Probably not until Monday," he replied, entering a passcode into the pad beside the door and pushing it open. They walked up to a counter where a uniformed man waited. He handed Grant a clipboard to sign the chain of custody, then pointed to another table where Mindy's belongings were laid out.

"Take as long as you need," Agent Wilcox told them. "Just text me when you're done and I'll escort you out." He left them to their search.

On the table were a suitcase and two plastics tubs that apparently held loose items from her cabin. Grant pulled vinyl gloves from a box on a nearby shelf and handed a pair to Kate.

"Let's start with the suitcase," he suggested. "And please take photos of everything as we go along. I'll make a few notes, but the photos will be more helpful." Kate donned the gloves and took out her phone.

The suitcase was a typical mid-size hard shell case in cobalt blue on casters. It was barely scuffed, so it appeared to be fairly new. Grant opened it up and spread it on the table. It was empty. He unzipped all the side compartments just to make sure. He closed it back up, and Kate took photos of the Alaska Airlines tags still attached to the handle: LAS to ANC.

He opened the first tub and began removing the items, all clothing, and laid them on the table. Kate dutifully took photos while he checked all the pockets and ran his hands over the garments searching for anything sewn into the seams. Next were the shoes. He removed all the insoles, finding nothing.

"All the same sizes, looking fairly new, actually." He indicated a dress still bearing tags from Macy's. After carefully returning everything to the tub, he put it under the table and opened the second one. This one would take more time. It held everything from cosmetics and toiletries to maps, brochures and a Kindle. Her purse was lying on top.

"I'm assuming the clothes she was wearing will be bagged and left in Anchorage," Kate remarked.

"Probably."

"Grant, look at this." She extracted a worn leather Bible with Mindy Marshall inscribed in gold lettering on the front. She began thumbing through it, noting the many portions highlighted with various shades from a colored pencil. Toward the back, a piece of paper acted as a bookmark in the Gospel of John.

Kate unfolded it and gasped.

"What is it?" Grant asked, coming to look over her shoulder.

"It's a DNA report. A paternity test, from a lab in Las Vegas. Arnold Caldwell is Mindy's father."

"Whoa, that's a wrinkle we hadn't considered!" Grant exclaimed. "Is it dated?" Kate had spread out the paper on the table and was taking a picture of it.

"August 3rd. Less than two weeks before the cruise." She stood back and looked at Grant. "I wonder if this is what she was going to talk to me about that night in the restroom?"

"More importantly, does Arnold know?"

They quickly went through the rest of Mindy's things, including her purse. Her phone had already been sent to the lab in Anchorage, but Kate took photos of her credit cards – there were only two – and 'Valued Customer' store cards. Her keys were hanging from an ornate wooden cross. There was a key fob for a Toyota, and two that appeared to be for buildings. Probably her condo, and the office.

They closed the tubs and signed off on the custody sheet. Grant texted Agent Wilcox, and he met them as they exited the Evidence Room. He was quite interested to learn of the DNA discovery, and Kate sent him the photo of the report.

"I was about to release the Caldwells and Dimarco so they could return home, but now..." They had exited the building and were standing on the sidewalk. "Now I'll have to come up with an excuse to detain them a little while longer."

"Maybe the phone records you're waiting on?" Kate suggested.

Agent Wilcox nodded. "That's about all I've got. And Caldwell is not going to be happy. He left me a message a few minutes ago while I was with you insisting he had to get back to Vegas for an important business meeting."

"Please call me as soon as you have those records, and we'll help you sort through them. I've done it before, and it's quite a chore."

"Thanks, you can be sure I'll take you up on that!" He shook their hands and said they would probably hear from him Monday.

Grant and Kate decided to walk back to the hotel, intending to find a spot in town to have a late lunch. They passed quaint shops offering works of local artists and craftsmen, including everything from jewelry and paintings to chainsaw-carved animals. They found a deli on a side street with tables out front, and liked what they saw on the posted menu. Breaking away from seafood, they decided to split a Reuben and sweet potato fries. The sun was warm on their backs, and a light breeze ruffled the umbrella.

"Well," Grant said as he polished off another French fry, "it looks like we're at a standstill until Monday."

"I just hope we learn something that makes more sense than what we've uncovered so far," Kate agreed.

"Mindy had to have been killed by somebody at the lodge, since it's so isolated."

"Exactly. There are no roads. The only access is by plane or boat. All the lodge employees – and that's only 9 or so – live in cabins on the property during the summer season."

"And we still have no real motive. I mean, why would anyone want to kill Mindy just because she's Arnie's daughter? Certainly not her own father!"

Kate sat back, tapping the table with her fingers. "Plus, we don't even know if he's aware of the relationship. Frankly, Julia would have more motive to eliminate an heir than he would."

Grant raised his eyebrows at that thought. But he couldn't visualize the socialite and non-profit volunteer being a murderer. Not to mention she was in the gift shop with several witnesses at the time of the attack.

"There's something else I was thinking about," Kate mused. "Something must have occurred for Mindy to even consider that Arnold was her father. From what Sal told us, she must have been researching her birth parents for a while. I wonder if we could locate any friends from college who might know?"

"Her ex-boyfriend would definitely be a place to start," Grant agreed. "See if you can track down who he is and his current whereabouts. At the very least, we can call him."

"Good idea. Let's head back to the hotel and I'll get started."

The only clue Kate had about the identity of Mindy's former boyfriend was what Sal had told them, that he was the quarterback on the college football team. Thankfully, college yearbooks were now available digitally, and it took her less than half an hour to locate him.

"Randy Kolchek," she exclaimed triumphantly to Grant. "According to his social media, he's married and works for a car dealership in Arizona." After a few clicks of her mouse, she called out the company phone number to Grant.

Grant dialed the number, and a woman answered, saying "Scottsdale BMW, how may I direct your call?"

"Randy Kolchek, please."

"One moment, I'll connect you." Grant placed the phone on the table, setting it on speaker.

"This is Randy, how may I help you today?"

"My name is Sheriff Grant Thompson from Napa, California, and I'm assisting in the investigation of the death of a former college classmate of yours. Do you have time to answer a couple of questions?" Five seconds of silence elapsed before he responded.

"Which classmate?"

"Mindy Marshall." They heard a distinct gasp.

"Mindy's dead? What happened?"

"She was killed while on vacation in Alaska."

"But...was...did she..."

"All I can tell you at this point is that her death was a homicide."

"I'm so sorry to hear that. She was... Mindy and I dated for a while before we graduated." It was obvious that the man was struggling to maintain his composure. "What can I answer for you?"

"We have reason to believe that Mindy was adopted. Did she ever discuss that with you?"

"Yes, as a matter of fact, she did. She was working with an organization online."

"Did she have any success in tracking them down?"

"I don't know...maybe. We...uh, we split up after graduation. I haven't really talked to her since."

They talked for another minute or two, but Randy didn't have any further helpful information, so Grant disconnected the call after requesting he contact him if he thought of anything else.

"Well," Kate sighed, "that raised more questions than it answered. Sal told us she'd said she was looking for her birth parents, not that she'd found them, or even had a solid lead. And Arnie told us he sought out graduating seniors looking for a replacement for Norma. Was it just serendipity? Or did one of them suspect the other was related to them?"

"Is that why Mindy interviewed with Arnie?" Grant asked. "Or is that why Arnie hired her?"

"More to the point," Kate said with another sigh, "does it really matter?"

CHAPTER FIFTEEN

Monday dawned with drizzly gray skies which apparently didn't dampen the spirits of the tourists. Sitting having breakfast in the hotel restaurant, Kate and Grant watched the raingear-clad passengers disembark from the latest cruise ship to arrive in port. The newlyweds had enjoyed a beautiful Sunday, putting aside the murder, and relishing in just being together.

Now it was time to re-engage in the investigation. Agent Wilcox had called early that morning, letting them know the cell phone logs had arrived, and the financial records should be there by lunchtime.

The agent met them in the lobby of the Bureau office and led them to a conference room. Folders were already lying on the table, and carafes of coffee and bottles of water were in the middle.

"All right," Agent Wilcox said as they all sat down. "The contents of each folder are identical. Grant, I know you've been down this road before, but I'm assuming you haven't, Kate?"

She shook her head indicating that this was new to her.

"Then let me explain what we have here. These reports are what is known as Call Detail Records, or CDRs. They show the destination phone number, duration of the call, start and end times, and the cell phone tower the phone was connected to." Kate realized how significant that last bit of information could be.

She flipped open her folder and glanced at the stack of papers. Each user's CDR pages were stapled together.

"What about text messages?" she asked.

"That's a bit more complicated," Wilcox replied. "The text messaging is shown in the CDR, but the contents of the messages are not. The complicated part is that the Caldwells and Sal all have iPhones, which are encrypted, and Apple doesn't have the ability to decrypt them. Mindy, on the other hand, had an Android, so we do have available the actual contents of texts from her phone."

"So, what's our plan of attack?"

"First, we'll highlight each of the user's phone numbers in different colors when they appear in a CDR of someone else." He motioned to a holder containing highlighters of four different colors. "Pink for Mindy, green for Julia, yellow for Arnie, and blue for Sal. Grant, you start with Mindy's CDR, I'll do Arnie's, and Kate, you take Sal's. Whoever finishes first can take Julia's. Then we'll tackle the unknown phone numbers that might be significant in our timeline."

Kate exchanged a glance with Grant as she took a handful of highlighters. This was no small task! Then, to try and make sense of it all...

One hour and two cups of coffee later, Kate had finally finished going through Sal's CDR. Grant, who wasn't new to this laborious process, was working on Julia's report. Kate took a bathroom break while the others finished their reports. When she returned, a secretary was setting out sandwiches on the table along with cans of soda and iced tea.

"Thank you both for helping," Agent Wilcox said as he began unwrapping a sandwich. "This would have taken me the better part of the day by myself."

"Glad to help," Grant replied, choosing a ham and swiss sandwich. "But now comes the hard part. Trying to tie them all together."

"Then let's start with the easiest – Julia's." He looked at Grant, who was flipping the report closed.

"She had no calls to Mindy, and no texts. Only three calls to Sal, none in the last week, and no texts. Surprisingly few calls and texts to her husband, and only one since the cruise began: on the afternoon of the murder. The call was not connected, but apparently went to voicemail."

"Can you tell where Arnie was when the call came in?" Kate asked hopefully. Wilcox shook his head.

"No, cell tower information is only available when a call is connected," he replied. "Based on the time of the call, Julia was probably calling him to let him know about the attack on Mindy...and that they wouldn't be able to rejoin the cruise."

The agent flipped through Arnie's CDR, locating an outgoing call. "Arnie called his wife about two hours later, pinging off a tower in Juneau."

"How about calls to or from Sal during that time period?" Grant asked. Kate had Sal's CDR, and scanned down to Thursday afternoon.

"No calls, but there was a text sent to Arnie. Content unavailable, of course."

Grant looked over at Wilcox. "Speaking of Arnie, were you able to verify his whereabouts the day of the murder?"

"To an extent," the agent replied. "Shortly after Mindy's body was found, Lieutenant Davis ordered Mr. Caldwell's phone to be pinged."

"Can you explain how that works?" Kate asked. "Is it like GPS?"

"In a way, but not as accurate. Law enforcement has the ability to send a signal to a cell phone without the user knowing it's being done. Signals are returned from the closest towers, and the triangulation of their locations shows the location of the phone."

"And where was Arnie when this was done?" Kate crumpled up her sandwich wrapper and dropped it into the paper bag from the deli.

"At a government office building in downtown Juneau," he replied.

Grant pulled out the email from Arnie he had printed after forwarding it to Wilcox.

"According to this, Arnie said he was meeting with someone from Alaska Salmon Hatcheries. Does that jive?"

Agent Wilcox slowly shook his head, and looked at the Thompsons.

"No, it does not. That company is located several miles away."

"Then who was he actually meeting?" Kate wondered. "And why?

CHAPTER SIXTEEN

A light knock was heard at the door, and the same secretary who had brought lunch entered with another stack of folders.

"Financial records," she explained, setting them down in front of Agent Wilcox.

"Thank you, Sylvia," he replied, parceling them out to Grant and Kate.

"One more thing regarding the CDRs before we dig into these," Grant remarked. "Were there any outgoing calls from Arnie on Wednesday or Thursday that could correspond to his meetings on the day of the murder?"

Agent Wilcox scanned through the CDR, and looked up.

"Yes, one call on Thursday afternoon at 1:20 to a number I recognize as a government exchange. Let me check it out." He pulled his laptop in front of him and entered the number into a law enforcement database.

"It's the office of a lobbyist, Lyle Scofield."

Grant sat up in his chair. "A lobbyist? Let me guess...the fishing industry?"

"No, actually he represents the gaming industry."

"Gaming?" Kate closed her eyes and thought back to one night at dinner on the cruise ship. Her eyes snapped open. "Grant, do you remember that night when you asked Arnie about Caldwell Industries? He said they were a conglomerate...and rattled off some of the products they manufacture. Didn't he mention the gaming industry?"

"Yes, he certainly did," he replied. "Along with the fishing industry and wind and solar generating equipment, I believe."

"Well, let's just verify what we've seen," Agent Wilcox said, pulling out his phone. Referring to the email Arnie had provided of his activities on the day of the murder, Wilcox dialed the number of Alaska Salmon Hatcheries. He asked for John Baker and was transferred to his secretary. He identified himself, and indicated he was confirming information in relation to an ongoing investigation.

"Did Mr. Baker have an appointment with Arnold Caldwell this past Thursday?" He put the phone on speaker so Kate and Grant could hear the conversation. In the background they heard paper rustling, probably pages of an appointment book.

"Yes, at 1:00. However, about ten minutes into the meeting, Mr. Baker was called away to an emergency at one of the hatcheries. I assume they intend to reschedule in the near future."

After thanking her, Wilcox disconnected the call. "And a few minutes later, Arnie placed the call to the lobbyist's office."

"What time was his phone pinged?" Grant asked.

"2:53," Wilcox replied. He glanced between Kate and Grant. "Should we find out what Arnie has to say?" They both smiled their replies.

Arnie answered on the third ring.

"Mr. Caldwell, this is Agent Wilcox. I'm here with the Thompsons, who have been helping me with the Mindy Marshall investigation. We have confirmed that you had a brief meeting with John Baker of Alaska Salmon Hatcheries early in the afternoon on Thursday. Could you tell us what you did after that?"

"Had a late lunch, then just strolled around town a bit. I saw I had missed a call from Julia, and called her back. That's when she told me what had happened at Taku Lodge, and that we were being put up in the hotel in town."

"Thank you, Mr. Caldwell. I think that's it for now." He disconnected the call, and sat back in his chair.

"Now, that's a red flag."

Arnie slammed his hand on the table, accompanied by a string of curses. "They're getting suspicious...I can smell it!"

Sal looked up from his phone. "Relax, boss, they don't know nothin'."

"Easy for you to say," Arnie scoffed. "And you're sure she didn't have it with her?"

"Nope, and like I told you, I went through everything in her cabin after we got back from that wilderness trip Wednesday, while she and Julia were in the spa."

"Okay, okay," Arnie said, running his hand through his hair. "Then it has to still be at her condo. Maybe even at the office. Damn, I wish they'd let us go home!"

CHAPTER SEVENTEEN

Agent Wilcox assigned the banking reports to be reviewed by the same individual who analyzed the CDRs. In addition, there was a thick folder for Caldwell Industries. Agent Wilcox put that aside to deal with last.

After working in silence for quite a while, Agent Wilcox spoke up.

"Finding anything unusual?"

"Not really," Grant replied. "Mindy's salary was direct deposit, and she routinely paid her bills on the 15th of each month. Of those two bank cards we found in her wallet, one is a debit card tied to her main checking account, and the other appears to be paid off each month. She also had a savings account, and automatic transfers occurred each month right after her salary was deposited. She also used an app to make donations to her church every month. Bottom line, no surprises."

"How about Sal's records?" Wilcox asked Kate.

"His account was opened just over four years ago, with a small initial deposit. So, it doesn't appear that he transferred from another bank at another location, and it's interesting the timing coincides with the lack of online history prior to 2018." Kate tapped her pencil on the paperwork. "He's not nearly as organized as Mindy, I must say. He also doesn't appear to be making payments on his condo. According to tax records, his unit was purchased for cash by this...uh...Diamond Investments."

Agent Wilcox wrote down the name of the company, and said he would ask Pamela Russell, the data analyst at the ABI, to dig into it.

After knocking lightly, Sylvia entered the room, laid a note in front of Agent Wilcox, and left. The agent quickly scanned the note and looked up, a grimace on his face.

"The local authorities in Las Vegas went to Mindy's condo today at our request and found it tossed. Contents of drawers and shelves dumped on the floor, wastebaskets upended, even the couch cushions slashed."

Kate and Grant exchanged a look of astonishment.

"Why on earth would someone do that?" Kate asked, "Unless...unless they thought Mindy had something valuable?"

"Or something incriminating," Grant added.

"This adds a new twist to our investigation," Wilcox stated. "Trying to determine a motive for Mindy's murder becomes even more challenging."

Grant threw down his pencil and tipped back his chair. "Didn't we determine that in her capacity at Caldwell Industries she coordinated with the accounting department?"

Kate nodded. "Yes, both Julia and Arnie mentioned that, and it was her minor in college."

"Then I think we need to focus on Caldwell Industries," Grant continued. "It's looking like Mindy may have been killed because she suspected something was fishy with the books."

Kate looked at Grant. "And that may have been the real reason she wanted to talk to me that night in the ladies' room. To ask for my help."

"I think it's time we have a conversation with Pam Russell," Wilcox announced.

Grant and Kate decided to stretch their legs while Agent Wilcox set up the teleconference with the analyst, whose office was at the Major Crimes Unit in Anchorage. Not wanting to leave the building, they wandered down a hall with historical photos of Alaska hanging on the walls.

"I don't know about you," Kate said, "but I'm loving Alaska. It's so ruggedly beautiful, not to mention huge! It would take several visits to really get to know it."

"I hear you...especially about its size. Hard to imagine, but there are about the same number of people living in San Francisco as in the entire state of Alaska!"

Kate moved down the hall, stopping at a photo of the Iditarod, the annual sled dog race. "If it wasn't for the long, cold winters, I wouldn't mind living here."

"Let's settle for summer vacations, shall we?" he laughed, drawing her into a side hug. His phone vibrated in his pocket, and he looked at the text message. "Wilcox is ready. Let's head back."

The flat-screen on the wall behind the conference table was on, revealing a young woman with spiked dark hair and a silver nose ring sitting at her desk. Agent Wilcox introduced Kate and Grant, then gave the data analyst a summary of what they had learned so far.

"Everything is pointing to possible irregularities at Caldwell Industries," Wilcox finished. "We need your help in digging into the organization and its subsidiaries."

The woman gave them a knowing smile. "Already on it. This organization is a bit like an onion: layer upon layer, many of them being shell corporations. Many of the companies are legit, of course, like the one that manufactures equipment for the salmon hatcheries. But others?" She smirked. "Buried quite deep is Diamond Investments. And they don't directly manufacture anything. They own a company that provides components to the gaming industry. And it's tied to the mob."

Grant frowned. "But I thought the Feds cleaned up Vegas more than twenty years ago."

"Oh, they did, pretty much. All casinos are corporate-owned, licensed and inspected by the Nevada Gaming Commission, and long gone are the days of mob bosses owning them."

"I hear a 'but' coming," Kate murmured.

The analyst laughed. "*But*, they just got more creative. The corporations are often linked to interests in Asia and Russia, with new spins on gaming, like cheating and marker schemes, not to mention financial fraud and cyber schemes."

"Then how do we determine if something illegal was going on with Caldwell Industries...something that Mindy might have stumbled on?"

The analyst shot a look at Agent Wilcox. "You might want to take a bathroom break," she hinted. He raised his eyebrows, but then stood and left the room with a knowing look on his face.

Pamela waited until the door clicked shut before speaking. "He doesn't need to officially be aware of some of my, um, investigative methods," she said. "I'll try to determine if there were accounting discrepancies, perhaps even two sets of books, one for the feds, and the other for 'internal use.'"

"Understand," Grant said with a chuckle. "But even if you find something, it wouldn't be admissible in court."

"True. But that's where you two come in. From what you've all been telling me, it sounds like Mindy had some hard evidence that someone doesn't want anyone else to find."

"Sounds like we all have our work cut out for us," Kate said.

CHAPTER EIGHTEEN

After a long day at the ABI, Grant and Kate were looking forward to a relaxing evening.

"I wonder how much more we'll be able to do here?" Kate said as she and Grant walked to a restaurant for dinner. Agent Wilcox had informed them that the Caldwells and Sal Dimarco were being allowed to return home the following day.

"Not much, I would imagine. It all boils down to solid evidence, which is sorely lacking at the moment." He was all too familiar with how quickly a case could turn cold.

They had chosen a favorite with the locals that specialized in King crab. The pub was tucked away on a backstreet away from the historic downtown, and the minute they walked in, they knew Wilcox hadn't steered them wrong. The décor was a blend of rustic and quirky, and they were seated at a table under a suspended dog sled. With so many tempting selections, they decided on crab bisque and a fisherman's platter. Grant chose a local craft brew, and Kate opted for a glass of white wine.

"This isn't exactly what we planned for our honeymoon, is it?" Grant laughed, toasting her with his foaming stein.

"Definitely a bit more of an adventure than the travel brochures mentioned," she agreed, lifting her glass to clink against his. "But I've enjoyed every minute of it. Napa is going to seem a bit boring, I'm afraid."

"Hold that thought," Grant said as he answered his ringing phone. It was Agent Wilcox – Grant wondered if there had been a breakthrough. After their short conversation, he disconnected and turned to Kate.

"Part Two of our honeymoon adventure coming up. Wilcox is sending us to Las Vegas."

"What?" she exclaimed. "Why?"

"He wants us to go through Mindy's condo with a fine-tooth comb. He thinks we would know better than the local police what might be significant to the investigation. And since Sal lives in the same complex..."

"A slice of surveillance on the side?"

"You got it. One floor of the complex has rental units, and he's secured one for us to use while we're there."

"When do we leave?"

"Our flight is tomorrow morning at 10:30. Have you ever been to Vegas before?"

"Unfortunately, yes."

He laughed at her response. "Not your kind of place, eh?"

"Definitely not! I was sent there a few years ago by the paper in San Francisco to cover a Star Trek convention." She rolled her eyes. "No comment."

"Well, I'm discovering all kinds of things about my new wife. But I have a feeling investigating a murder will rank higher than Trekkies."

She wrinkled her nose and spread her napkin on her lap, ready to tackle the crab legs.

* * *

The sun was low in the western sky when the Alaska Airlines flight banked for its final approach to the Las Vegas airport. To Kate it seemed incongruent to see skyscrapers rising from the desert floor. Especially the replica of the Eiffel Tower. Thankfully, they wouldn't be bombarded with the noise and lights of the 24-hour city, since Mindy's condo was located in the bedroom community of Henderson. They parked their rental car in the circular drive in front of the main building of the four-building complex, then walked into the tastefully decorated lobby and approached the rental desk. Grant rang the bell on the counter, and soon a middle-aged woman appeared from a room in the back.

"Mr. and Mrs. Thompson checking in," he announced.

"Welcome," she replied, setting a registration form in front of him. "Just fill this out for me, and you'll be all set." She pulled two key cards from a box, programmed them, and slid them into an envelope. "Room A220. I was also instructed to give you a key to room B415. It's the building just out the back door and to your left. You can park anywhere in the lot behind the complex."

Grant completed the registration card, put the key cards in his pocket, and turned to leave. He paused and turned back.

"Would you happen to know about security cameras in the complex?"

She narrowed her eyes and looked him over. "You're working with the police on that break-in, aren't you?"

"Yes, ma'am. And it would be helpful to review any security footage that's available."

"No problem. Stop by in the morning, and we'll have a look at it."

After Grant moved their car, he and Kate took the elevator to the second floor, and located their suite. It was a one-bedroom efficiency, with a small kitchen and dining area in addition to a good-sized living room. The unit overlooked the grassy courtyard between the buildings.

"Not bad," Kate commented. "Only drawback is there's no room service," she laughed.

"I spotted a shopping complex down the street, so I don't think we'll starve," Grant replied, pulling her into his arms and giving her a tender kiss.

"Mmm...more of that later," she said teasingly as she stepped back. "I don't know about you, but I'm itching to look at Mindy's condo."

"Yeah, me too. Let's check it out while it's still daylight. Then we can find some dinner."

They quickly unpacked their suitcases and went back downstairs, taking the stairs this time. Building B also had a small lobby, with seating areas and a bulletin board where condo announcements and neighborhood events were posted. They took the elevator to the fourth floor, and turned left to 415. Police tape was still stretched across the door, and after inserting the key card, he lifted the tape so Kate could duck under and enter the unit.

There was a box of vinyl gloves beside the door, and Grant pulled out two sets, handing one to Kate. Kate already had her phone ready, and began taking photos. Even in its trashed condition, she could tell this had been a well-decorated space. Soft grays, accented with muted blues and splashes of yellow carried through the two-bedroom unit. But whoever had gone through the rooms had left nothing untouched. Furniture overturned, cushions slashed, artwork torn out of their frames, books pulled off the built-in shelving units... and the kitchen was no less a disaster. Drawers were dumped onto the floor, food items pulled from the pantry, even the ice bin in the freezer had been tossed into the sink.

"What a mess," Kate groaned as she picked her way carefully through the piles of trashed items and broken glass to the main bedroom. More of the same greeted them. The queen mattress had been stripped of the bedding, and the box spring slashed open. A jewelry box was dumped on the floor, clothing was pulled from hangers, drawers upended...

Kate stooped and picked up framed photos that had probably been on the dresser and nightstand. One was a family grouping around the Christmas tree that she recognized from Mindy's social media of her parents and older brother, with his wife and two children. Another photo obviously taken on a ski trip showed her and a man, possibly her former boyfriend, Randy Kolchek. It was hard to tell considering the ski hats and goggles.

Grant was searching the master bath when they heard a knock on the front door. Thinking it might be the police, he went to answer it. But it was a young woman, nervously clutching a tote bag to her chest.

"May I help you?" he asked.

"Hi...yes, I'm a friend of Mindy's. Patty Sinclair. I...I live down in 423, and..." she suddenly burst into tears, and Grant gently pulled her into the room. He muscled an overturned couch upright, and guided her to sit down. Kate came and sat next to her, handing her a tissue she had retrieved from a crushed box on the floor.

"My name's Kate, and this is my husband, Grant. He's a Sheriff from California, and we were on the cruise with Mindy..." The tears started afresh, and Kate stooped and picked up the smashed Kleenex box, yanking out another tissue.

"I...I can't believe she's dead," Patty sobbed, *"murdered..."* She hiccupped and looked back and forth between Kate and Grant. "But I think she was afraid something might happen to her. She...that's why she gave me this before she left for the cruise." She pulled a MacBook Air out of the tote bag and set it on her lap.

Kate took in a sharp breath and looked at Grant. Was this what the intruders were looking for? It had to be!

Grant took out his small notebook, opened to a blank page, and handed it to her with a pen. "Patty, please give me your contact information. We're staying in A220 while we help the authorities investigate your friend's murder." While she scribbled down her name and phone number, he dug out one of his business cards and handed it to her.

Kate took the laptop and opened the lid. It came to life, displaying a mountain scene. The cursor blinked, awaiting the password.

"Any idea what the password is?" she asked Patty. The young woman pushed back her long blond hair and gave a half-hearted laugh. "I kept telling her to change it, but... it's Randy2018." Her former boyfriend's name and the year they graduated from college. Kate entered the characters and hit the return key, unconsciously holding her breath. Moments later, she was in!

"Well, I'm glad Mindy didn't take your advice," Grant said with a grin. "This will probably take us some time to examine, so we'll need to keep it for a while. Are you okay with that, Patty?"

"Absolutely," she replied, wiping her eyes with the tissue. "Whatever it takes to find out who did this to her."

"What else can you tell us about Mindy?" Kate asked gently. "Was she seeing anyone?"

Patty frowned. "Some guy from work kept hanging around. Big guy. But I don't think she was really that interested."

"What's his name?"

"Sal...something. And he lives here, too, so he was always making excuses to stop by."

That confirmed Kate's impression that the relationship was one-sided.

"Thank you, Patty," Grant said. "You've been very helpful, and please call me if you can think of anything else that might be important." She nodded and stood, folding up the canvas tote bag and handing it to Grant. Kate walked her to the door and gave her a brief hug as she left.

"Well, that was an unexpected gift," she said, shaking her head in amazement. "I can hardly wait to find out what she has stored in there."

"I know. Now we might finally get some answers. Let's take it to the rental desk and ask them to lock it up in their safe before we go to dinner." Kate handed him the laptop and he placed it back in the tote bag. He paused to send a quick text to Agent Wilcox, letting him know of their discovery, and that they would be in touch again in the morning.

CHAPTER NINETEEN

"Yeah, they just left. And he was carrying something in a bag. I don't know how my guys missed it, but *they* obviously found it." Sal watched Grant and Kate exit Building B and walk back to theirs. Sal paced back and forth in front of the window in his unit in Building D, directly across the courtyard from Mindy's building. He hated that he had to call his boss, but he'd had no choice.

"I don't have to tell you what needs to be done," Arnie said in a grim voice. "And we're running out of time. Don't mess it up this time!"

Arnie resisted slamming the phone down on his desk, and kicked the wastebasket instead.

Sal was sweating when he bounded down the stairs of his building and darted over to Building A. He cursed when he saw Grant hand the tote bag to the woman behind the rental desk. He hurried back to his condo, and quickly put in a call.

"The sheriff and his wife must have found what you were looking for, and it's now in the condo building safe. They'll probably take it to the feds to hack into it, so you need to stake out Building A, and make sure they don't get it delivered. Got me?" His tone left nothing to speculation about exactly what he meant. He began pacing again, and suddenly wondered if Kate and Grant would try to access the laptop themselves. He decided he'd better tail them when they left for dinner just to make sure.

* * *

Grant retrieved the laptop the next morning, and took it back to their rental condo. On their way back from dinner the night before, they had stopped at a grocery store to pick up some basics. The coffee maker was gurgling, and a pot of steel cut oatmeal was bubbling on the stove. Kate poured glasses of orange juice and set them on the breakfast bar.

"You realize I'm forcing myself to eat breakfast first," she said as she watched him place the laptop on the table.

"I get that, honey. But you may be at it for a while, and I can't have my bride collapsing from hunger."

There was a knock at the door, and Grant cautiously went to look through the peephole. "It's Sal." He barely had the door unlatched when Sal charged him, knocking him flat on his back on the floor. Before Kate had a chance to even scream, two other thugs rushed in, slamming the door behind them. One man, wearing a tank top that revealed full sleeves of tattoos, grabbed Kate, holding a gun to her head, and shoved her into a dining room chair.

"Not a peep, lady, or your man will never father children."

The other man, who sported a scraggly beard, pulled Grant to his feet so Sal could bind his wrists with zip ties. Sal shoved Grant onto the couch, and bound his ankles with more zip ties. Grant glared at the man, sorely wishing he had brought his weapon with him. He looked at Kate, who had a terrified look on her face. Tattoo Guy had a grip on her hair, and the muzzle of this gun at her temple. Bearded Guy took over for Sal, aiming his gun at Grant. Sal strolled over to the table and stroked the laptop.

"Ah, finally." He turned and addressed Tattoo Guy. "Bring her over here. Let's see what Mindy was hiding."

Kate was yanked to her feet, wincing as the thug pulled her by her hair towards the table. He pushed her into the chair in front of the laptop and let go of her hair, but still pointing his gun at her head.

"This won't do any good," she protested. "The laptop is password protected."

Sal scoffed. "Maybe so, but if you didn't think you could hack your way in, you would have taken it to the police, and not brought it up here." Kate looked at Grant, and he gave her a slight nod. He wasn't about to risk her life for forged company records.

Kate's stomach was roiling, and she tried to calm her nerves as she lifted the cover of the laptop. She realized there was no point in pretending she didn't have the password. Three men with two guns would win the day. She typed in Randy2018, and brought up the home screen.

"See, I knew you could do it," Sal said with an obnoxious sneer.

"Why don't you just take the laptop and leave us alone?" Grant asked hopefully.

"Now what fun would that be? After I confirm that what I'm looking for is on it, I *will* be taking the laptop...and my friends here will be taking you two on a lovely drive into the desert."

Kate choked back rising bile, and looked at her husband of less than two weeks. He sucked in a breath and clenched his jaw. *Lord, please help us!* Turning back to the laptop, she clicked on Documents and scrolled down the list of folders and files. She began methodically opening them all, especially the spreadsheets, realizing the file names could be deliberately misleading.

Nothing.

Then she came to a file entitled Journal. It was a Word document, and when she opened it, she discovered it was exactly that – Mindy's journal, covering the last three years or so.

"What did you find?" Sal asked, leaning over her shoulder to look at the screen.

"It's just her journal. And it's over a hundred pages."

Irritated, he slapped the table.

"Read it. There has to be something!"

Biting her tongue, she typed 'Caldwell' in the search field, and advanced through all the instances found in the document. The first few were from her initial interviews with the company, and when her new boss was mentioned. But then she came to an entry from June 15, two months prior. She quickly read through the post.

"I found something."

Sal was at her back, his breath on her neck.

"What's it say?"

"Mindy mentions that she found proof of double sets of books, and Arnold Caldwell attempting to bribe a state senator in Alaska to spearhead bringing traditional gambling to the state."

"Yes!" Sal was jubilant.

Until Kate interrupted him.

"But she writes that she transferred the evidence off this laptop onto a USB drive. She was afraid someone suspected she knew what was going on."

Sal was livid. "That little...I knew I should have taken care of her sooner!"

Not that it mattered now, but Grant realized Sal had just admitted to killing Mindy.

Just then, the smoke alarm in the kitchen began emitting its deafening, shrill warning, and everyone jerked to look. The pot of oatmeal on the stove was sending up a black cloud.

In a split second, Grant had pulled his knees up and thrust his legs out, kicking Bearded Guy in the gut, sending his gun flying across the room.

Kate took advantage of Sal's momentary distraction, jumping up and giving him a karate chop, knocking him into Tattoo Guy and toppling them both.

Grant raised his arms and brought them quickly down on his leg, breaking the zip tie on his wrists, and then he dove to the floor, grabbing Tattoo Guy's gun.

He rolled and aimed it at Sal.

Kate retrieved Bearded Guy's gun and pointed it at him.

Five minutes later, the fire department arrived.

CHAPTER TWENTY

Grant and Kate were escorted by Special Agent Daniel Hicks to the viewing room next to the interrogation room at the Las Vegas FBI office. Sitting across from two agents was a very uncomfortable-looking Arnold Caldwell. Gone was the air of confidence and the politician-perfect smile. In its place was a man with disheveled hair, wearing a rumpled suit and undone tie. It looked like he had slept in his clothes, because he had.

Expecting to put out a fire, the Las Vegas fire department had arrived the morning before to find the occupants holding three men at bay with guns. The police were quickly summoned, and after rescuing the smoldering oatmeal and turning off the smoke alarms, the firemen departed.

The once cocky Sal Dimarco had immediately rolled over on his boss, confessing to the murder of Mindy Marshall in exchange for a plea deal to turn state's evidence against Arnie Caldwell. The CEO was arrested in his office in downtown Las Vegas, and warrants were forthcoming for the books of Caldwell Industries.

The FBI had been able to answer Kate's question as to why there was no online presence for Sal prior to 2017. He had been serving a 10-year sentence in prison on RICO charges under his legal name of Sal Ferraro. His father, Stefano, had indeed been from Arnie's neighborhood in the Bronx, and asked his childhood friend for a favor when Sal got out of prison.

The agents interrogating Arnie were grilling him not only on his connections to the mafia in New York, but also his involvement with lobbyists in Alaska and bribing a state senator.

"What were his intentions?" Kate asked as they listened.

Special Agent Hicks replied. "There's no lottery in Alaska, and the state only allows Class II tribal casinos to offer bingo and pull-tabs." Seeing the confusion on her face, the agent explained. "Pull-tabs are similar to scratch tickets in other states. Anyway, one of Caldwell Industries' legal subsidiaries manufactures gaming machines, and he was trying to persuade this senator to introduce legislation to permit traditional gambling. Agent Wilcox will be pursuing that aspect of the investigation."

Grant joined the discussion. "I suppose that company, and other legitimate ones, like the one that supplies products for the salmon fishing industry, were just coverups for illegal activities?"

"Exactly," Special Agent Hicks replied. "We've only begun scratching the surface so far, but we expect to uncover money laundering schemes, online gambling, loan shark activities, and more. We believe Mindy had found documentation proving those illegalities, and that's why she was murdered."

"I can't help wondering what happened to that USB drive," Grant said.

"Actually, I think I know where it might be," Kate replied, pulling out her phone. She scrolled through the dozens of photos she had taken of Mindy's personal effects in the evidence room in Juneau. Finding the one she remembered, she showed it to Grant and Special Agent Hicks.

Grant frowned. "The key ring? I don't get it." Kate used her fingers to zoom in on the photo.

"See that tiny crack below the arms of the cross? It pulls apart, revealing a USB drive."

"And just how do you know that?" he challenged.

"Easy," she chuckled. "I saw it listed in Mindy's orders on Amazon." Grant burst out laughing and gave her a high-five.

"I'm going to call Wilcox and have him check it out. Whatever's on there will help the investigators know what to look for when the warrants are issued."

Just then, Kate shushed them and turned back to the one-way window. "I just heard one of the interrogators mention DNA."

Special Agent Hicks turned up the volume on the speakers.

"...found this lab report in Mindy's Bible. Were you aware she was your daughter?"

What little color was left in Arnie's face drained and his mouth dropped open.

"M..my daughter? *Mindy?*"

"Yes, records indicate she had been working with an organization to find her biological parents, and a woman answered an inquiry. Although she wished to remain anonymous, she mentioned she had been a prostitute in Las Vegas and became pregnant after visiting the hotel suites of men at a convention for the gaming industry. She saw name badges with 'Caldwell Industries' and began researching the company."

Words tumbled over each other as Arnie tried to formulate his thoughts.

"But...the interviews. I...when Norma retired, I went to UNLV. The business school. Mindy was there..."

"According to her journal, she was determined to get hired at your company. After she did, it took her over three years to conclude you were probably one of the men at that party twenty-five years ago. She collected samples from three men, and one came back as a match. Yours."

Arnie seemed to shrink into his chair. Tears were running down his cheeks, and he made no attempt to wipe them away.

"Have you...does Julia know?"

"Not yet. We'll leave that conversation for you to handle."

Kate turned from the window and looked up at Grant.

"I realize he's hardly an upstanding citizen, but I have to admit I feel a bit sorry for him..."

Grant nodded, looking over her shoulder into the interrogation room. "Seriously. I can't imagine living with the reality that you authorized someone to kill your own child." He looked at Special Agent Hicks. "Thank you for allowing us to be here this morning. But if there's nothing else we can answer at the moment, I think we'd like to get on with our honeymoon!"

"Absolutely, Sheriff Thompson, and as they say, we know where to find you. This investigation will probably take several months, but I'm sure we'll be calling upon you both in the future for depositions."

Grant and Kate were escorted back through security, and were soon standing in the hot noon sun of Las Vegas in August.

"Well, Mrs. Thompson, what do you say we blow this joint?"

"Looking forward to getting home, that's for sure. I'm just sorry we didn't get to finish our Alaska cruise."

"Ah, but remember we were given a voucher from Princess towards a future cruise. So, let's start planning our first anniversary trip!"

"Hopefully with a little less drama," she laughed as they walked hand in hand towards their car. As Grant was opening Kate's door, his phone rang.

"Hello, Clark, what's up?" He listened to his Chief Sheriff for a few moments, and Kate had a sinking feeling when she saw the look on his face. "All right, we'll be back later today; I'll meet you at the office for an update." He disconnected the call, and stowed the phone in his pocket.

"Another threat to Ariana. Her dog has been poisoned."

THE END

About the Author

Jane describes the gift of writing as painting a picture with words. She enjoys plots with unexpected twists, mixing genres and taking the reader on a journey, but always with a Christian worldview. A stickler for accuracy, she incorporates her characters into the fabric of actual historical people and events, providing the reader with a window into bygone eras.

Other Books by the Author

Visit the Author's Page at:
www.amazon.com/author/janeritzenthaler
and her website: www.janeritzenthaler.com

Made in the USA
Las Vegas, NV
27 April 2022